BOSWELL'S
LUCK

BOSWELL'S LUCK

G. CLIFTON WISLER

M. EVANS
Lanham • Boulder • New York • Toronto • Plymouth, UK

Published by M. Evans
An imprint of Rowman & Littlefield
4501 Forbes Boulevard, Suite 200, Lanham, Maryland 20706
www.rowman.com

10 Thornbury Road, Plymouth PL6 7PP, United Kingdom

Distributed by National Book Network

British Library Cataloguing in Publication Information Available

Library of Congress Cataloging-in-Publication Data

The hardback edition of this book was previously cataloged by the Library of
Congress as follows:

Wisler, G. Clifton.
  Boswell's Luck / G. Clifton Wisler.
    p. cm.—(An Evans novel of the West)
  I. Title. II. Series.
  PS3573.I877B67   1989
  813'.54—dc20

ISBN: 978-0-87131-611-0 (cloth : alk. paper)
ISBN: 978-1-59077-262-1 (electronic)
ISBN: 978-1-59077-261-4 (pbk. : alk. paper)

♾™   The paper used in this publication meets the minimum requirements of
American National Standard for Information Sciences—Permanence of
Paper for Printed Library Materials, ANSI/NISO Z39.48-1992.

Printed in the United States of America

For R. Ellwood Jones, Jr.
mentor and friend

Chapter One

Day broke slowly over the mesquite-studded hills that spread out beyond the Brazos River. The faint golden glow crept wearily over the distant horizon, its warming rays seemingly kept at bay by cruel phantom fingers that perpetuated the midnight bite of a razor-sharp north wind. Springtime in Texas was an unreliable season, like as not to freeze or burn a man as it chose. Or so it seemed to the solitary figure leading his horse through the rocks above the river.

Another man might have found the going hard, even impossible. The Brazos hills had only recently been wrested from the Comanches and reclaimed from the buffalo. Big-boned longhorns and spotted mustangs shared the ravines and rock slides with rattlesnakes and wolves. Oh, a few foolhardy men tried to make a go of it growing corn or running beeves, but even they waited for daylight before tackling the treacherous hills.

Many a cowboy had lost his pound of hide to mesquite thorns or suffered from the sharp needles of pencil cactus.

Erastus Hadley paid such perils little mind. He'd taken his first steps on that very hillside, and even before that he'd ridden behind his father's broad back atop a shaggy pinto, scaring up range ponies or collecting stray calves at roundup. And if a mesquite limb battered a cheek or shoulder, what of it? Pain was an old acquaintance, after all.

"We're here, boy," he whispered as he dropped the horse's reins, leaving the animal to graze idly while he continued climbing the rocky slope. Even a mule would be pressed to reach the crest without snapping a tendon or cracking a bone. Loose rock soon had Erastus crawling on hands and knees up the steepest section. A river of dislodged sandstone rocks cascaded below, sending a pair of deer scampering for cover. The hillside was reached quite easily from the north, for the ruts of the old Overland Stage route came down from Ft. Belknap that way. Erastus wasn't looking for easy paths, though. No, he'd come the old way, as he had with the nimble-footed legs of youth.

Then, as now, he'd come to spy the tree, the giant. The biggest white oak to be found for maybe a hundred miles. It was a ghost tree, some said, possessed of spirits and haunted by night. In the faint predawn light the old tree appeared more than ever enchanted, for its eerie ivory branches waved in the wind most frightfully, casting dark shadows across the chalky hillside. The moaning of the wind had been enough to send Erastus running twenty years ago. Now, though, the tree held a different sort of power over Erastus Hadley. As he leaned on a large boulder and wiped the cold sweat from his forehead, he gazed at that enormous oak and sighed. Spring hadn't brought any green sprouts this year. The old ghost tree was dying—was dead already most likely.

"Just as well," Erastus grumbled. It seemed appropriate. For more than anything else on that rock-hard stretch of earth, the white oak represented folly—the kind of misplaced trust and hope that brought a man to bury his dreams—and his friends, too.

It hadn't always been that way, though. A decade before, Erastus Hadley had ridden to the white oak as a wild-eyed, snaggle-toothed boy of fourteen. With hair bleached white by a summer sun and a shrill voice that betrayed approaching manhood, Rat Hadley was pure terror on horseback.

"Hard to tell where the horse stops and the boy begins," old Orville Hanks had remarked to J. C. Hadley.

Hearing the gruff rancher's pronouncement, Erastus had tipped his hat and charged out down the trail.

"Boy's got his pa's way with the horses," Payne Oakley, the ranch foreman, said that same evening. "Be a good hand. He's got a nose for findin' mustangs, and he don't scare 'em away."

"Oh, they think he's one o' them," a cowboy remarked. "Kind o' takes on their smell, don't you think? Not that I'm high on bathin', mark you, but a fellow has a hard time o' it ridin' by Rat there when the wind turns his way."

"You could use a scrub, you know," Mitch Morris had added in a whisper. "Maybe we ought to sneak on down to the river and have a swim. Be good to shed some o' this blamed Texas dust."

"Dust?" Erastus cried, slapping his hat at Mitch so that a sandy cloud descended on the other youngster. "Can't call this dust. You been in town too much lately, Mitch. This is just a saltin' o' sorts. Real dust comes, and you change colors twice at least."

"Well, you want to swim or not?"

"Wouldn't mind," Erastus confessed, grinning at his friend. "Race you down there?"

"If you can catch me," Mitch replied, darting around a juniper and dashing toward the Brazos a quarter mile beyond.

It wasn't much of a contest, actually. Mitchell Morris spent too much time in town, where his folks ran the mercantile. Whole days he passed on the center bench at Mr. Barley's schoolhouse, reading and doing ciphers. Mitch was winded halfway, and Rat raced past spouting taunts and flinging off dusty clothes on his way to the rocky pool where the hands swam away the dust and fatigue that came with hunting mustangs.

"Lord, I wonder sometimes if you aren't half pony yourself, Rat," Mitch said when he finally arrived at the river. "Nobody ever outran you anywheres."

"Don't see why some try."

"It's the stubborn streak Ma says I get from Pa," Mitch declared as he undressed. "And there's the odd chance you'll run into a beehive or a nest o' nettle."

"Yeah, there's that," Rat confessed.

And there was that other, unspoken truth. As the eldest son of a restless cowboy, Erastus Hadley had few calls to take bows. He was short on size, and his pinched-in face and long, thin nose were as responsible for his nickname as the similarity to his actual name. Mitch, who was taller and already thought handsome by some of the town girls, could look down the trail to a fine future. He was quick with figures, and his winning smile drew folks to him like honey. As to Rat Hadley, well, the road would have been rough anyway. It seemed that fate singled out the Hadleys for special trials.

Just then, though, Rat was splashing in the river as he might have with his little brothers, a yellow-haired wisp with a hide tanned leather tough by sun and circumstance. Mitch, by comparison, seemed almost civilized. His sandy-blond hair was trimmed neatly, and his flesh had yet to take on its nutmeg summer tint.

"Two more weeks chasin' range ponies's sure to remedy that," Rat suggested between splash battles. "Make you seem a regular sort o' fellow 'stead o' some starchified schoolboy."

"Ain't my notion passin' time in a schoolhouse," Mitch barked.

"Beats plantin' corn or mindin' brothers," Rat grumbled. "Anyway, we got half the spring and all summer to run down mustangs or help with roundup. And next year Mr. Hanks is sure to want me along for the drive to Kansas. Maybe he'd take you, too."

"Good help's hard to come by," Mitch added.

"Is when you won't pay a wage," Rat said, sighing. "But it does give a boy or two the chance to sign on. I hear some high tales 'bout Dodge City, Mitch."

"Sinful town, Ma says. Keep us busy the rest o' the year askin' forgiveness. But I 'spect it'd be worth it."

Rat grinned shyly, then motioned toward a log floating near the far bank of the river. In an instant the boys took off through the water. But Mitch's long arms and steady strokes were of no use. Rat plowed up the river as he thrashed his way to the log.

"Here I thought you could swim, Mitch!" Rat cried gleefully.

"I'll show you what I *can* do," Mitch answered, grabbing Rat and pulling him along to the muddy bank. The youngsters wrestled for a good ten minutes before Rat wriggled free. He then rinsed off the mud and began collecting his clothes.

"Best we get along to the line camp," Rat called. "Pa's not one to wait dinner on anybody, 'specially not with Mr. Hanks and Payne along. Mornin's a long time comin' on an empty belly."

"Sure is," Mitch agreed. And so they returned.

That night after supper Rat sat with his back to a boulder and listened to his father strumming chords on a battered Mexican guitar. Soon the horse hunters gathered for a bit of singing. The youngsters among the crew joined in for a bit before rolling out their blankets and shutting their eyes. The solemn music blended with the chill wind, and Rat threw a second blanket over Mitch before doing the same for himself.

"Cold night," Mitch observed.

"Look at the sky," young Eduardo Mota added. "Is the devil's moon up there. A bad omen, amigos."

"Just a full moon's all," Mitch argued. "No devil to it."

"No, you wait and see," Eduardo insisted. "Bad luck. See the clouds go by? My sister Isabella die on a night just like this. Bad luck always follows the devil's moon."

"Go to sleep, Eduardo," Rat said, laughing. "Make sure you check yer cinch tomorrow. Many's the cowboy fell off his horse when the devil's moon came a-huntin'."

Mitch imitated a coyote's howl, and a pair of the regular cowboys took it up.

"Is bad luck to make fun o' the spirits," Eduardo complained. "Very bad luck."

Perhaps it was, Rat thought later. But just then he was fourteen and full of beans and vinegar, as his mother liked to say. He loosened Eduardo's cinch personally, and the young wrangler took an early tumble. Soon, though, Rat spotted the tracks of a dozen or so unshod ponies. In no time the whole outfit was galloping after a small herd of range ponies, intent on driving them down a nearby wash and along into a box canyon.

"Cut 'em off, Rastus!" J. C. Hadley yelled to his son. "The big white! He's the leader!"

Rat slapped his horse's rump and sliced his way through the flank ponies until he could glimpse the big white. It was a marvelous horse, a world of muscle and fiery independence determined to retain its freedom. As Rat broke past a brown mare, he balanced himself carefully, tied the free end of his lariat to his saddle horn, and raised a loop with his right hand. Racing close, he threw the loop high, and it fell cleanly over the nose and head of the stallion. In seconds the rope went taut, burning Rat's fingers as it tore away from his grasp. The boy slowed his mount and waited.

"I got you, horse!" Rat screamed as the rope twanged, and the big white rocked to a halt. The fiery-eyed horse turned its head and screamed. Its scarlet eyes turned toward Rat with a hateful gaze as the big horse struggled to work its way free of the confining rope. Rat's own horse wobbled unsteadily. Then, as the white made a fresh try at freedom, the speckled mustang lost its footing. Crying wildly, Rat grabbed the rope as the knot tore loose from his saddle horn.

"Let go, boy!" Payne Oakley urged. But it was too late. The white stallion jerked Rat high into the air and then dragged him fifty feet through a nest of rocks, scrub juniper, and prickly pear. Rat yelped in pain as his arms were scraped raw and the bottom was near scraped off his trousers. He managed to fling the rope at a mesquite tree, and the knot obligingly caught in a crook and held fast as the others rode in to take charge of the defiant stallion.

"Lord, Rat, you went and got yourself a cactus baptism!" Mitch called as he hurried over to his friend. J. C. Hadley wasn't far behind. Rat gazed at his bloody arms, at the cactus spines peppering his thighs, at the bare skin exposed by his tattered britches, and gazed up with a smile.

"Got the horse, Pa," he explained.

"Near the other way 'round," J. C. observed. "But I admit you caught him. Now all that's left is mendin' you and breakin' him!"

Rat nodded. With Mitch's help, he set about tending to the first task. His father and Payne Oakley turned to the other.

That same afternoon, standing bare-chested and wearing patched trousers, with daubs of brown herb concoctions marking near every inch of exposed flesh, Rat watched as his father attempted to harness the raw energy of the wild white stallion. If there was a grander horse on earth, Rat couldn't imagine where it might be. Men for miles around rode out to have a look.

"I tell you not to mock the spirits," Eduardo whispered as he joined Rat and Mitch outside a makeshift corral that enclosed the open end of the box canyon. "You don't believe the devil moon."

"I got the horse," Rat boasted. "Now Pa's going' to break him."

"Maybe so," Eduardo said, pointing to the frothing horse. "Maybe not. He has the devil's eyes."

"What's this?" Mitch cried. "Devil's moon. Devil's eyes!"

But Rat motioned for his friend to be silent. Mitch hadn't read those fiery eyes. J. C. Hadley was more'n a match for any normal horse. But for the first time Rat began to worry. The big white calmed for a moment, and J. C. threw one leg over the demon beast and settled atop it. Then the big white exploded.

"Lord, lookee!" Payne shouted as he scurried clear of a flying hoof.

"Madre Maria," Eduardo said, crossing himself as he hopped back from the corral.

J. C. Hadley bounded high in the air, but his powerful hands maintained their grip on the stallion, and he settled back onto the horse. Twice more the horse bucked its would-be conqueror, and again after that. J. C. dug toes into the big stallion's ribs, and the horse whined and stomped. Then, with a flurry of wild spasms the white raced full speed at the corral.

"Pa, look out!" Rat cried as the stallion slammed into the gate and staggered back. Shaken, J. C. lost his grip. The horse threw itself at the fence now, shattering a foreleg and rolling onto one side. Hadley jumped, but the big horse rolled onto his legs and over his back. Rat heard the crack of bones and yelled to the men scrambling over the walls of the corral. Payne Oakley was already leveling a pistol at the horse's head, and two rapid shots left the stallion limp and quiet. Meanwhile others dragged the fallen horse off their luckless friend.

"Let me by!" Rat shouted as arms reached out to hold him back. "Pa?"

"Rastus, boy, he's smashed up proper," Payne argued as he gripped Rat's sore, battered arms. "You don't want to . . ."

"He's my pa," Rat insisted, breaking free. "I seen him as bad as a man can be."

"No, you haven't," Mr. Hanks said, stepping in front of Rat. "His back's broke, son. He won't even know you."

"I'll know him," Rat said, slipping past the men and making his way to where J. C. Hadley lay coughing out his life. Blood trickled from his mouth, and a world of pain flooded the horse-breaker's eyes.

"Rastus?" J. C. muttered.

Rat nodded, then picked up his father's limp hand and gave it a squeeze. "Pa?"

"Mind yer ma, son," J. C. managed to whimper between moans.

"Was blind hate, Pa," Rat said, gazing a second at the fallen horse. "Pure meanness. You had him licked, and all he knew to do was kill himself and hurt you in the bargain."

"Hurt you, too. More'n you'll know for a time."

"I'll mend," Rat assured his father.

"Time for crossin' over now," J. C. whispered as he formed the first note of a hymn on his lips. He tried to hum it, but he managed only another moan. The assembled wranglers pulled off their hats and took up the melody, and a familiar glow filled J. C.'s eyes. Then it was gone.

Chapter Two

All men have sad days if they live very long. If Erastus Hadley lived a thousand years, he'd never know a time to equal the fiery hot April afternoon when he rode alongside the wagon bearing the broken body of his father homeward. Never had a boy felt as alone, as lost.

Actually, he wasn't alone, though. Orville Hanks was driving the wagon himself, and Payne Oakley rode a sorrel just ahead. Mitch Morris had come along, too. But none of them knew quite the words. . . . Perhaps there were none.

It was on toward three o'clock when they finally approached the plank cabin Hanks had built ten years earlier to watch the eastern fringe of his acreage. For five of those years J. C. and Georgiana Hadley had made the line camp into a sort of home—at least as much as was possible for a vagabond cowboy.

"Got to have some kind o' roots," Georgiana had declared. "We got four youngsters now, and I won't live forever out o' saddle bags, J. C.!"

Erastus recalled the conversation well, being nine by then. At the time it seemed strange that a man might need more than a creek to swim or range to ride. Now, though, that rickety cabin was home and as good a place as he'd ever known.

Oakley moved ahead in hopes of seeking out Georgiana and preparing her for the news, but she was seeding her garden and spied the wagon.

"J. C.!" she called. "Rastus?"

Hearing his name called swept Erastus's own grief from his mind. He nudged the pinto out of line and sadly approached his mother. Words formed on his tongue, but they refused to come when he opened his mouth.

"We brought you some hard news," Oakley finally spoke as he joined them.

"How bad's he hurt?" she asked, staring at the wagon.

"Horse fell on him," the foreman explained. "Didn't feel any pain, ma'am. Was over quick."

"Rastus?" she asked, turning to her son. "That the truth of it? I never knew a horse to throw my man."

"It was a devil," Erastus said, dropping his eyes. "Ran me through the brush when I roped him. Didn't throw Pa. Ran him right into a corral fence. Kilt the horse to do it, but the thing didn't seem to care."

"That's how it was, all right," Oakley agreed. "Craziest thing I'll ever see. No ordinary horse could've killed J. C. Hadley. He was the finest man atop a horse I ever knew."

"We'll put him on the hill, under that stand o' live oaks," Georgiana instructed. "He'll always have shade, and there'll be birds to sing. He was fond o' singin'. Rastus, you find the spade and see to it."

"I'd deem it a favor if you'd leave that to me ma'am," Oakley said. "We all o' us thought well o' J. C. I expect Mr. Hanks'll have somethin' for you, but the boys all pitched in what they could, and I'd have you take it with our respects."

"Thank you, Mr. Oakley," she answered, nodding somberly as the foreman handed over a kerchief that jingled with the sound of silver and copper coins. "Spade's out back o' the shed. Rastus, you take Mr. Oakley's horse, will you? Then best fetch your brothers and sister. They'd be seein' to the corn."

"Yes, ma'am," Erastus replied. He then set about his assigned tasks and left his mother to master her grief.

Finding Payne Oakley a spade and seeing the horses tended was the easy part. In fact, the work kept Erastus from thinking of more serious matters. Mitch pitched in, unsaddling the Hadley horses while Erastus pumped fresh water into a trough.

"My pa always says the Good Lord makes things hard to test us," Mitch said when Erastus satisfied himself that the needs of the animals had been met and turned toward the creek.

"Figure Marcus needs testin', do you?" Erastus asked, kicking a rock past the barn as he imagined how the news would strike his seven-year-old brother. "Ain't the heat and the raw wind enough? Ain't there 'nough rattlers and fevers to kill you without sendin' killer horses?"

"Just tellin' you what Pa says is all, Rat."

"Maybe that talk holds for town folk," Erastus replied angrily, "but out here we know the Lord's got better things to do than bother a fellow. It's the devil's taken my pa, sure as day! And ole scratch's 'bout finished me, too."

"How's that?" Mitch asked, grabbing the smaller boy by the arm.

"Best let go, Mitch," Erastus warned. "I got a powerful urge to thrash somebody, and you'd be awful handy."

"Go ahead and wallop me if you think it'll help. Sure don't seem like I'm doin' you much good as is."

Erastus shook loose of Mitch's grasp and scowled. There was a world of torment choking Rat Hadley, and not a thing Mitch said would lessen it a hair. Erastus hung his head and stumbled off to locate his brothers and sister.

They were at the edge of the cornfield, splashing their feet in the creek. Usually Erastus would have run into their midst and howled at them for neglecting their chores. Instead he muttered a greeting and searched to find words to share the dread news.

"Somethin's wrong," eleven-year-old Alex announced. "Ras?"

Eight-year-old Juliana read the sorrow in her oldest brother's eyes and burrowed under one of Erastus's arms. Little Marcus huddled between her and Alex.

"Pa's dead," Erastus told them. "Kilt by a devil horse. Got to go up to the house now. There's men buryin' him. We'll be sayin' our good-byes and readin' the prayer book."

"You ain't joshin', are you?" Alex asked.

Erastus shook his head, and Mitch did the same. Marcus stared up in dismay, and Juliana buried her head in Erastus's side and wept.

"Go ahead and cry, the three o' you," Erastus advised. "'Cause we'll be back with company soon, and won't Ma allow it. Mournin's private. I recall her tellin' me that when we buried Grandpa Sullivan down on the Colorado."

"I never knew Grandpa Sullivan," Juliana sobbed. "I loved Pa."

"Me, too," Marcus added.

"Then get to cryin'," Erastus barked. "Get it out o' yer system. 'Cause we'll do none o' it at the buryin', hear?"

"I hear," Alex said, wiping his eyes and taking Marcus in hand. "Don't you got any tears to shed, Ras?"

"Not with folks 'round to see," Erastus said, nodding to Mitch. "'Sides, cryin' won't change a thing."

The others sighed as if to agree, but they wept a bit longer. Erastus left them beneath a stand of junipers and drew Mitch aside.

"Best you leave us to ourselves a bit," Erastus said. "You been a good friend to help bring Pa home."

"You want me to leave?"

"Nothin' left for you to do, Mitch. Ain't nothin' to the buryin'. You come back in a day or so. Maybe we'll chase up some more ponies. Leastwise we'll have ourselves a swim."

"Mr. Hanks'll think hard o' my leavin'."

"No, he's a man for workin'. Truth is, he'll be back at it himself in two hours' time."

Mitch hesitated, but Erastus waved him along. Shaking his head, Mitch Morris set off toward the barn. Erastus joined his brothers and sister.

The Hadley youngsters were a whole hour wringing the tears out of their hearts. Afterward Erastus led the way back to the cabin. They were only halfway when they passed the lonesome hill overlooking the creek. Georgiana waved them to where Oakley had dug a shallow grave in the rocky ground. With hardly a moment's pause, she motioned to the still shape now wrapped in a patchwork quilt.

"Pa?" Juliana asked.

"Only his earthly remains, darlin'," Georgiana Hadley replied. "Say your 'byes, dears, and hold your tears. We got words to read and prayers to make. Your Pa's gone on to his reward, bless him, and we got our own worries."

Those words were prophecy, as it turned out. The last words of a hymn had hardly melted in the fierce afternoon heat, and Payne Oakley was only shoveling the first sand over J. C. Hadley's corpse, when Orville Hanks motioned Georgiana and Erastus down the hill a way.

"I feel like I've lost my own right hand," Hanks declared, slapping his hat against his thigh. "Lord, this is hard luck."

"Harder on us, Mr. Hanks," Georgiana answered.

"You know J. C. and I soldiered together," Hanks went on. "The one or the other o' us pulled the other out o' more bad spots! Why, I owed J. C. my hide more'n once. But just now I can't be thinkin' on that account. Ledger's closed, so to speak, and life marches on to the next campaign."

"Yessir," Erastus said, searching for some meaning behind the words.

"You understand, Georgiana, I built this ranch out o' rock and sweat. I lost hundreds o' critters off this east range 'fore I put up the line camp. J. C. did a fair job o' . . ."

"Fair job?" Georgiana asked with wild eyes.

"More'n fair, to tell the truth. I paid him fair, too. Took on his oldest when I had the work. Would've seen Alex a cowboy, too, if the years'd been kind. But now I got to tend to business. I need a man out here I can trust to watch my stock, to see we don't lose none to rustlin' nor fire, either. Only right I should offer that man this cabin."

"How long, Mr. Hanks?" Georgiana asked sourly.

"Be two weeks 'fore we finish gettin' the horses together and another to start roundup. Three weeks," Hanks concluded.

"And I've got that much time to find work and settle my family?"

"It's all I can offer."

"Well, it's fortunate J. C. was a friend. Elsewise we'd be leavin' in yon wagon, I'm sure."

"That's not called for," Hanks argued.

"I'm not in an apologizin' mood, sir!" she stormed. "I'd deem it a favor if you'd leave me to look after my little ones. You have horses to break, I believe. I'll send Erastus along later."

"No, keep him to help you," Hanks argued.

"We'll need the money, sir," Erastus explained.

"I'll pay you, boy, but it's your ma needs you now. Stay here and help her. You got some big shoes to wear now your pa's gone. Take some doin', bein' J. C. Hadley's son."

"Always has," Erastus answered.

Late spring wasn't the best of times to look for work. Not with planting done and most of the male population readying themselves for the long cattle drives to Kansas. Georgiana Hadley did her best to find a place for her fatherless family, but Thayerville was the only town close by, and they had a seamstress and a café already. Oh, odd jobs could be had, but hardly at a wage to feed four growing youngsters, much less provide shoes or britches. Georgiana lacked the aptitude for dealing cards, and she didn't have the easy manner or shapely figure of a saloon girl.

In desperation she sent out frantic telegrams, hoping some friend or relative might come to her aid. In truth, there was pitiful little family left after the war against the North and the Comanche raids that had killed her own two brothers. Finally an answer came from her mother's sister down in Austin.

"Good news?" Erastus asked as her mother scanned the sparse words.

"Partly," Georgiana answered with a frown. "Alex, Juliana, Marcus, you three hurry along a minute. Look after the hens. I've got words to share with your brother."

"Can't we know, too?" Juliana complained. "He always gets to know first."

"Hush!" Georgiana scolded. "Now off with you."

Alex took his little brother and sister by the hand and pulled them outside. Once the children had gone, Georgiana motioned Erastus to her side.

"Is it about me?" he asked.

"About all of us," his mother explained. "Aunt Cordelia has a rooming house in Austin. Two of her grandchildren live there with her, but they're young. She's offered to take me on as cook. Juliana can help, and Marcus is the same age as her little grandson Crane."

"What about me and Alex?" Erastus asked.

"She's found a place for Alex to work. He'll be looking after horses at a nearby stable, and he'll take his meals and pass his nights with us."

"And me?"

"Cordelia says," Georgiana began. She paused to swallow a tear, then scanned the telegram again. "Cordelia feels you're old enough to find your own way."

"I promised Pa I'd look out for you," Erastus objected. "I swore I would."

"We'll be just fine, Rastus."

"Then why're you cryin'?"

"Because I don't like to think what's in store for you. I was on my own at fifteen, and it wrinkles a body so you think he's twenty goin' on forty. Makes for an early grave, son."

"I'll get by."

"I'm of a mind to tell Cordelia no," Georgiana said, clasping her eldest son's hand. "It's a hard thing, comin' o' age with no father to lean on. Alex and Marcus'll need you. Juliana, too, in a different way."

"And you?"

"Yes, me, too. If only there was some other other way . . ."

"Isn't, though, is there?" he asked, "I heard Miz Cathcart talkin' how we're sure to be taken into an orphan's home. Or else split up and sent off to this farm or that. Aunt Cordelia'd keep Juliana and Marcus with you, and Alex . . . well, he wouldn't be far."

"You would."

"I might could find work in Austin."

"I wouldn't think that likely, Rastus. If there was anything handy, Cordelia'd found it."

"Maybe Mr. Hanks'd take me on the drive?"

"I asked already," Georgiana said, pulling him closer. "I guess I've spoken to near every farmer or rancher for twenty miles."

"I'm fourteen, Ma!"

"And better'n nigh any full-grown man I know. But they all say you're thin. And smallish, after my people. I tell 'em how you work, but they all ask why Orville Hanks doesn't take you in then."

"Wonder so myself."

"There's one man'd take you in," she said nervously.

"The Morrises? Wouldn't be so bad livin' with Mitch. He's close to a brother."

"Otto Plank," she muttered.

"Ole man Plank?" Erastus asked, feeling his legs wobble. "He beats his horses, and his boys, too, to hear folks talk, Ma, I'd as soon take my chances in Austin."

"And how would you get there, Erastus?"

"Ride my horse."

"Your horse? That pony doesn't belong to you, son, no more'n this cabin or the creek. Everything's Orville Hanks's property."

"I'll walk."

"No, I'll write Aunt Cordelia and send my regrets. I couldn't sleep knowin' you were out walkin' the wilds, food for wolves or target for Comanche arrows."

"Ain't any Comanches out here anymore. I got a talent for fishin', and I got a good eye with a rifle. Wouldn't go hungry."

"I won't go unless I know you've got a roof over your head, Rastus."

"Ma, I really ought to look after you and the little ones."

"We'll be all right. I'll see even Marcus writes you a letter every week."

"Wouldn't be forever, would it? I mean, I wouldn't have to stay if I didn't like it."

"No, and Mr. Hanks promised to keep an eye after you. By next summer you'll have some growth, and he's certain to take you on."

"If it just wasn't the Planks. That man's mean."

"He's promised to be kind," Georgiana assured him. "I'll speak with the Morrises, too. Perhaps they can come by and take you to Sunday meetings. That'd give you and Mitch some time."

"Yes, ma'am."

"Then you're agreeable to it, I take it?"

Erastus rubbed his chin and studied his mother's hopeful eyes. He'd promised his father to see to her needs. Wasn't that what he was doing, staying with the Planks so she and the little ones could go to Austin? His insides grew cold at the notion of living under Plank's iron fist, but he nodded his consent. After all, how bad could things be?

It wasn't long before telegrams flashed south to Austin and back north again. The last Sunday in April Georgiana drove her family toward Thayerville. In the open bed were three trunks full of the family's meager possessions. It didn't seem a lot to show for the good years they'd shared at the Hanks line camp.

The wagon halted but twice on its way into Thayerville. The first time was at the river crossing where a Methodist circuit preacher held the county's biweekly meeting. The final stop was in front of the ramshackle house where Otto and Virginia Plank made their home.

"Got to go now," Erastus announced as he tossed a flour sack filled with his father's razor, a good skinning knife, and two patched cotton shirts onto the hard ground. He gave Juliana a good hug, wrapped a spare arm around a sobbing Marcus, and gripped Alex's wrist.

"Be missin' you awful," the eleven-year-old whimpered.

"No, you'll be too busy with the horses," Erastus argued. "You got to be the big brother now. It's a hard job, but you'll do just fine at it."

"We won't stay little forever, Ras."

"No, we won't," Erastus agreed. "Then we'll get the bunch o' us together and talk over old times. Likely we'll have some tales to swap then."

"You take care o' yourself, Ras."

"Look after Ma and the tadpoles."

"Do my best at it," Alex promised.

Erastus darted over and gave his mother a parting hug. Then he stepped back and somberly waved good-bye. He imagined how tall they'd all be next time they were together. Why, he'd hardly recognize them!

"Won't be long till you come down for a visit," Georgiana called. "Mr. Plank promised you five dollars a week and Sundays off."

"That right?" Erastus asked, turning to where Otto Plank stood on the porch.

Plank said nothing. Instead he waved and grinned good-naturedly. Once the wagon resumed its journey, the balding farmer limped over beside Erastus and clamped a hand onto the boy's shoulder.

"Got yer farewells done wit?" Plank asked.

"Yessir," Erastus answered.

"Best. For now on, you got no fambly. Jest work."

"Sir, it's Sunday," Erastus objected.

"Won't be once you shed that good shirt and kick off them shoes. Then it be jest like the rest o' the days, with plenty to fill it up."

"But you promised Ma . . ."

"Don't you sass me, boy!" Plank shouted, backhanding Erastus hard across the forehead. "Boy eats my food, he puts in a day's labor. Now get yerself ready. And keep yer 'pinions to yerself. Hear?"

Erastus nodded sourly, and Plank cuffed him again.

"Best you unnerstand, boy. Yer ma offered you to every man from here to Mexico, and nobody else spoke up. She's off to her new life, and she's shed herself o' you. World starts and finishes with Otto Plank now, and if you don't want worse'n my hand on you, you take it to heart."

"And yer promises to Ma?"

"Oh," he said, laughing. "She didn't believe 'em anymore'n I did. You do as I tell you, you'll eat well enough. Maybe in time, I'll even find you some pocket money."

"And if I don't?"

"Man's got a right to shoot a boy who tries to steal a horse," Plank said, grinning. "Won't be a soul to say otherwise. No neighbors for miles, you know. Unnerstand how it be?"

Erastus nodded bitterly. And that very moment he determined to show Otto Plank his heels the first chance that came along.

Chapter Three

The opportunity for escape didn't come. What did were hours and hours of back-breaking work that left Erastus haggard and blistered, little more than a ragged, barefooted slave.

To be truthful, Erastus wasn't alone in his suffering. Otto Plank had four boys of his own. Peter, who was nearly seventeen, shared the barn loft with Erastus and fourteen-year-old Efrem. The younger boys, Randy and Veston, spread their blankets in an empty stall down below. The whole bunch were locked in the barn by night, and there wasn't a one of them escaped their father's harsh words or ready hand. At the slightest sign of rebellion, the old man would take a rawhide strip to the back of the offender.

Once, when young Veston dropped a china plate at breakfast, Plank bent the child over a chair and whipped him raw.

"That's 'nough!" Erastus cried when he could stand Vesty's howls no longer. "Cain't you see he's bleedin'?"

"I can see I got to find another chair," Plank growled.

The other boys scurried for cover as Plank headed for Erastus. For a moment he only waited. The scowl on Plank's face and the upraised strap struck terror. He hadn't been raised to shy from trouble, but he knew the sting of that strap, and he couldn't help retreating.

"Where you goin', Rat?" Plank called. "Rat! That's what they call you, ain't it? Gutter rat. Own ma wouldn't even take him. Ingrate! Don't you know more'n to talk back to your betters!"

"Betters?" Erastus shouted. "You may be bigger, but you ain't better. Why if Pa hadn't . . ."

Erastus never finished. Plank reached out and threw a chair out of the way. Then, like a pouncing wildcat, the big farmer was on the boy. The strap stung Erastus's neck and shoulders. He flinched as it ripped open his shirt and tortured his ribs.

"How's it feel, Rat?" Plank howled as he laid on blow after blow. "I'll teach you some respect."

"Pa, no!" Peter called. "You'll lame him. Won't be no good to us then!"

"Please, Otto," Mrs. Plank added as she fought to calm the shivering Veston. "You'll kill him."

Plank turned toward his wife a moment, then tossed the strap aside. He lifted Erastus by the chin and gazed hard into the boy's defiant eyes.

"You'd like to kill me, wouldn't you?" the old man asked. "Well, you'll be a long time buried 'fore you have the chance."

The words had the ring of truth to them. While Peter and Efrem dragged him along to the barn, Erastus shuddered from pain and shock. And also from the notion that he would live out his days on that accursed farm.

Seven days a week Erastus labored slopping hogs, feeding chickens, chopping kindling, and tending the fields. He rarely lifted his eyes past his feet, and he spoke only when the barn door was bolted and Otto Plank beyond hearing. Even then he rarely joined in the boastful jabbering of the Plank boys. No, he kept his vengeful dreaming to himself.

The sole bright spots in an otherwise grim existence were the infrequent visits of Mitch Morris and his folks. The first two Sundays Otto Plank met their questions with claims that Erastus was ill. The third Sunday Mrs. Morris would not be put off by excuses.

"It's the Lord's day," she declared. "That boy should be at meeting."

"Lord ain't payin' him!" Plank barked.

"You promised his mother he'd attend Sunday meeting," she complained, "and I promised her I'd look in. If he's still sick, best we take him into town for some doctoring."

"You take him, you keep him!" Plank replied.

"I've a notion we should've offered in the first place," Mr. Morris answered. "My boy's been by your fields. Says you've worked Rastus skinny and beaten him to boot."

"He's a headstrong boy and needs a firm rein."

"Then he's done a lot o' changin'!" Mitch yelled. "Where is he?"

"Where I put him!" Plank yelled. "Now get yerselves off my farm. I'll tend my own business. You tend yours!"

Erastus watched it all through cracks in the barn wall, but the door remained bolted, and he was a prisoner yet. The Morrises left reluctantly. They didn't let the matter lie.

Those next few days as Erastus bent himself to Otto Plank's will, he couldn't ignore the sense of being watched from afar. Twice while chopping weeds in the cornfield he saw a shape dart through the trees a hundred yards away. Once he thought he heard his name called. Then one morning after emptying a bowl of foul mush that passed as breakfast, he noticed Mitch Morris sitting atop a horse a hundred yards away.

"Rat! I come to take you to town!" Mitch called.

Otto Plank heard the words and rushed outside cradling a twin-barreled shotgun.

"Make a run for it and I'll chop your legs from under you," the big farmer warned. "And I'll do the same for that yellow-haired jaybird up yonder."

Erastus took a glance at Mitch and studied their chances. If he were to make a lunge at Plank, make him fire the shotgun, there might be a prayer.

"He'll do it, too," a sour-faced Peter said, stepping over beside Erastus. "You ain't been the first hand we had here."

The fearful look in Peter's eyes erased all notions of escape. A shotgun wouldn't leave much of Erastus Hadley, and Mitch would be poorly rewarded for his efforts by like treatment.

"Get clear o' my place!" Plank then shouted, firing one barrel in Mitch's direction. Mitch was well beyond range of the scatter-gun, but the blast unsettled his pony. Erastus gave his friend a disheartened wave, and Mitch rode off.

By late afternoon Mitch was back. Not alone, either. Sheriff Lem Cathcart led the boy along the fringe of the Plank cornfield. The lawman rested a pistol across one knee, and he seemed in no mood to tolerate any nonsense.

"Mornin', Sheriff," Otto Plank shouted as he hurried over to where Erastus and Efrem were laboring to wedge a stump from the ground. "Visitors's mighty rare. What can I do for you?"

"If what I expect's true, you can go straight to perdition!" the sheriff replied. "What's this I hear from Mary Morris 'bout you holdin' the Hadley boy against his will?"

"Pure lies, Sheriff," Plank said, eyeing Erastus nervously. "Boy's mother 'dentured him to me. I feed him and give him a place to bed down. He's like my own son."

"Judgin' by what folks say, that's a poor return for his labors," the sheriff countered. "Young Mitch here says you fired off your shotgun at him yesterday when he stopped by to visit."

"Well, I fired into the air, Sheriff. You know how life is on a farm. There's never time to get everything done. If I let my neighbors do it, they'd have the boys off swimmin' and fishin' every day. I can't feed the seven o' us without clearin' this new section. Can't do that alone."

"That the way it is, Rastus?" the sheriff asked, glancing past Plank to where Erastus leaned against the defiant stump. "You just out to fool away the day with Mitch?"

Erastus started to reply right away, but he noticed Otto Plank plunge one hand in his right pocket. The old man favored carrying a pocket pistol, and the sheriff was certain to catch the first bullet. And afterward . . .

"I did have work," Erastus answered. The sheriff glanced back at Mitch, and Erastus felt his heart die. There would never be any escaping the old man now. Never! It seemed like his insides went all cold and hollow. He felt his fingers tremble.

"Ask him 'bout the beatin's," Mitch yelled accusingly. "I seen it with my own eyes. Look 'neath his shirt, Sheriff. There's welts left."

"Some boys need a hard hand now and again," Plank muttered. "I take a boy in, I expect him to walk the straight and narrow."

"Lemme see your back, Rastus," Cathcart called. "I got children. I expect I can judge what's fit handlin'."

"That's a father's job," Plank objected.

"He ain't his pa!" Mitch shouted.

"Shut up, boy!" Plank warned as he moved over and let the hidden barrel of the pistol fall upon Mitch's angry face.

"Now that's funny," the sheriff said as he slid down from the saddle. He then reached out and grabbed Plank's hand. The pistol discharged, blowing a hole in the farmer's overalls and sending a ball into the adjacent live oaks. "None too friendly, Plank," Cathcart added as he pried the pistol from the old man's fingers.

"You got no business here," Plank grumbled as he stepped back from the steel-eyed lawman.

"Rastus?" Cathcart called.

Erastus stumbled over to the sheriff's side. It was all he could do to steady his legs. The sheriff held his pistol on Plank with one hand and squeezed Erastus's shoulder with the other.

"Show him your back, Rat," Mitch urged.

Erastus stared hatefully at Plank, then wriggled out of the oversized shirt and stood bare to the waist. Cathcart frowned as he stared at the pale, emaciated skin stretched over Erastus's ribs. Then, turning Erastus slowly, the sheriff scowled at the sight of the long, whitish scars and the fresher red ones left by the rawhide strap.

"Veston, boy, come over here and show off yer own back!" Plank barked. The youngster hurried over and stripped off his shirt. The sheriff studied the criss-crossed scars and wiped his forehead.

"Ain't a thing under the sun I can do 'bout how you handle yer own boys, Plank!" Sheriff Cathcart declared. "Till you kill one o' them anyhow. But I'll not see you turn a whip to Rastus here."

"Suit yerself, Sheriff," Plank said, grinning. "Take him along. I got no use for him anyhow. He ain't worth a nickel. You know wasn't another man in the county offered to take him in."

"Well, it may be that'll change," Cathcart replied. "As to you, I'll put charges together so you answer a judge, Plank."

"What charges?"

"Well, to see Rastus here, I'd say attempted murder on him, not to mention that bitty matter o' aimin' a pistol at me. Should have gone right on and shot you, I expect. Done the world a service. Just between the two o' us, I might happen along out here in a week or so, maybe bring my boy so he can swim with your youngsters. If I see any fresh whip marks,

I might have a bit o' a huntin' accident, maybe shoot you through the head. You understand me?"

"You can't talk that way to me, Sheriff! I got witnesses. Peter, Efrem, Veston, Randy, you boys heard."

"Did they?" Mitch asked. "I wonder if they'd remember."

Erastus turned to gaze at Vesty. The boy was buttoning his shirt, but the hateful gaze directed at his father was not to be missed.

"Rastus, you climb up on that horse with Mitch there," Cathcart instructed. "I'd judge it best you come along with me."

"Where?" Erastus asked.

"Jail, to start with," the sheriff explained.

"Jail?" Erastus cried. "I done somethin' wrong?"

"Not anything I seen," the lawman said, laughing at the boy's wide eyes. "It's just I got a tub there we can use to scrub you up. Cora's mighty sour on company comin' to dinner without washin'."

"Sir?"

"I figure to put some o' Cora's chops in you, Rastus. You're too old to have folks countin' them ribs, son. And we'd be sore put to explain your britches slidin' off in the middle o' Front Street."

Mitch offered his hand, and Erastus gripped it. With one foot in the stirrup, Erastus managed to climb up onto the back of Mitch's pony. In moments they were riding toward town—and away from the Plank place and what Erastus Hadley would always envision as hell come to earth.

Chapter Four

Ordinarily Erastus had little use for bathtubs. In point of fact there were
whole stretches of the frontier that had never seen one of the contraptions.
If a body were to get tired of the dust or sweat Texas could heap on him,
he found himself a creek or a river and washed himself. Now, though,
with more folks turning to town living, somebody or other was apt to purchase one from a mercantile catalogue.

Erastus had heard of them. His father once told how at trail's end a hundred cowboys would line up at the bathhouses in Abilene or Dodge City
to have a turn at a tub. After soaking in perfumed soap, they'd deck themselves out in new boots and fresh duds so as to enjoy the favors of the
town's female population. Erastus and Mitch had quite a hoot listening
to the tale. Later they swapped boasts of one day joining the drives and
lavishing their attentions on the prettiest girls in Kansas.

It was just talk, of course. Erastus had a fair amount of trouble exchanging words with the Delancy girls at Sunday meeting or even looking at pretty Heather Hanks without turning redder than a beet. So when he found himself turned over to Sheriff Cathcart's twelve-year-old daughter Becky at the jailhouse, he was struck completely dumb.

"Well?" she finally asked. "Pa says I'm to bring you soap and carry off them rags you call clothes. You can fetch the water your own self. Won't be warm comin' straight from the pump and all, but it's too hot to light up the stove, and I never knew a boy to care much 'bout warm water anyway."

"Give a lot o' boys baths, do you?" Mitch asked, grinning.

"Well, I scrub my brother Busby regular. Or near to regular anyway."

"He's just seven," Erastus pointed out. "I'm twice as old."

"Twice the bother, too," she observed. "We had bigger men'n you in jail here, you know. I get 'em washed."

"Well, you ain't washin' me," Erastus insisted. "Mitch can bring you my clothes. We'll fetch the water. You give me the soap now."

"Pa says I'm to see you wash," the girl argued.

"Well, you cain't do that without seein' a whole lot more, and ain't that goin' to happen, hear?" Erastus barked. "Now git."

"He means it," Mitch added, opening the door and prying the soap from her hand. "Becky, ain't any winnin' arguments from Rat Hadley, either. He's stubborn as a bottomland mule. I'll bring you his rags in a bit."

"All right. I'll be by later on, though," she said, turning toward the door. "If I don't smell somethin' better'n ole cow dung, I'll just keep the clothes and leave you to soak."

"I'll bet she will, too," Mitch said after closing the door on her. "She's sure to ride herd on some poor fellow one o' these days. Lord help the fool."

"Yeah?" Erastus asked. "I always thought she was kind o' pretty."

"Fallin' in love, eh?" Mitch asked, laughing as he turned his attentions to the pump. "Well, there's fresh trouble for you. Sheriff finds out you're messin' with Becky, he's sure to turn you back over to Plank."

"Just might," Erastus said, forcing a smile onto his face in spite of the wave of pain such a thought brought. He then dragged the tub into the back room and began carrying the filled buckets of water there. In short order the tub was half full. Erastus then shed his clothes and hopped into the tub. The water was cold, but it felt refreshing in the hot, stuffy storeroom. And as he washed away the accumulated grit, it seemed he was also ridding himself of pain and grief.

It was hard to believe one boy could carry so much filth on his body. When Erastus abandoned the tub and wrapped himself in a linen sheet Mitch had set on a chair, the water remaining in the tub was little more than a muddy swill. As for Erastus, scrubbed pink he looked thinner and more wretched than ever.

"Lord, didn't they feed you at all, Rat?" Mitch exclaimed. "Ain't anything to you."

"Give me a few o' Miz Cathcart's chops. I'll fatten up."

"Be a time doin' it. I tell you, Rat, I close to found me a rifle the day that ole man fired off his scatter-gun. I was of a mind to shoot him if the sheriff hadn't come."

"Like as not you saved my life, Mitch. I won't be forgettin' that."

"Good. Ma says I'm sure to need friends, what with my habit o' findin' trouble."

"Yeah? I got the same talent."

They shared a laugh. Then Mitch handed over a wrinkled old shirt and a pair of patched trousers.

"Not too good a fit, eh?" Mitch asked as Erastus draped the shirt over his bony shoulders. "Were mine till I started this last batch o' growin'. I'll ride out and see if maybe Tommy Newton might have some things he don't altogether need. Be tomorrow, though."

"Cut me a length o' rope for a belt, and they'll do," Erastus suggested. "Later on maybe you can find me some drawers, though. These britches itch somethin' awful."

"Yeah, Ma uses a heavy dose o' lye when she washes. I generally give my things a rinse off under the pump 'fore I put 'em on."

"I'll do the same in the future."

They might have talked away the day had not Sheriff Cathcart popped through the door.

"Well, that's a considerable improvement," he announced. "Got some old boots here, Rastus. Give 'em a try. I'll judge you're tired o' goin' about in bare feet."

"You get used to it in the wilds," Erastus answered. "Thank you, Sheriff. Don't know how I'll pay you back."

"Was Mitch's ma brought the boots by, son. As to thanks, well, we're all o' us feelin' shame-faced from seein' your back. Your ma had our oaths that we'd look in on you. Didn't do too fine a job o' that, I'm thinkin'."

"Wasn't your job. I'm of an age to be my own lookout."

"And you'd likely done a fair job o' it if not for Otto Plank. Hurry into those boots now. Cora'll have supper ready soon."

Actually, though, before accompanying the sheriff to his house on the outskirts of Thayerville, Erastus had to pass Becky Cathcart's inspection. He felt a little like a horse at auction, what with her sniffing and staring and mumbling to herself.

"Your hair's all tangled," she announced, "We'll have to get it clipped. You got knobby fingers, too."

"Figure to cut them off as well?" he asked.

She smiled a bit and waved him on to the house. He got a kinder reception there from Cora Cathcart and little Busby. Mrs. Cathcart gave him a warm, motherly hug and offered her regrets at his ill treatment. Busby brought him a carrot to munch on and pleaded to see the scars on Erastus's back.

"Pay you a nickel," the boy whispered. "More if I had it."

"You come swimmin' with me and Mitch sometime," Erastus answered. "See 'em then."

As for the dinner, Erastus could hardly believe his eyes. Platters of pork chops and mounds of potatoes appeared before him. Vegetables he'd dared not dream of were piled high atop his plate. He'd been hungry so long he'd near forgotten what it was like to be otherwise. Now, as he gobbled bite after bite, it seemed he was bone empty and would need a year's eating to fill up.

"Pa, look at him," Becky complained.

"Take your time, Rastus," the sheriff instructed. "It's not goin' away, you know."

"Leave the boy alone," Cora scolded. "Lord knows what he's suffered. Forgive his manners this once."

Erastus grinned sheepishly and tried to be a bit more patient. His stomach would not be put off, though. It wasn't until he'd finished off his fifth chop and two platters of potatoes and vegetables that he untucked his napkin.

"I've got a peach pie set aside for later," Mrs. Cathcart announced. "Just now maybe you'd like to take Erastus into the sitting room, Lem. The children and I'll clean up."

"I can do my part," Erastus offered. "I've washed dishes aplenty and scrubbed a floor or two as well."

"Not this night," the sheriff declared. "Come along, son."

They strolled together out of the kitchen and along to a small room in the front of the house. Sheriff Cathcart placed a firm hand on Erastus's shoulder, and the boy looked up. Not since J. C. had the life crushed from him had Erastus felt anything but alone. Now it seemed there might be someone to ease the path ahead.

A knock came to the door then, and the sheriff motioned Erastus to a nearby chair and went to answer. Moments later John and Mary Morris joined him in the sitting room. Mitch, all scrubbed up and stiff-collared, followed slowly.

"Sheriff," Mr. Morris said, "we came to ask after Erastus. Have you thought of his future?"

"There's time yet," the sheriff answered.

"Have you work for him?" Mrs. Morris inquired.

"No, ma'am, but I can use a boy to sweep the jail house, and there are things here and there."

"We've done considerable thinking on this matter," Mr. Morris went on. "It's no service to provide sanctuary for a child only to turn him out later unprepared to provide for himself."

"We've a counter needs tending," Mrs. Morris added. "I hired a girl last month, but she's needed to help me sew garments. Mitch went out and filled a spare mattress with fresh straw, and he declares he needs a body to sleep on it."

"We got room, Sheriff," Mitch declared. "Shoot, we're together most days anyhow. Half the county already thinks us brothers."

"Rastus, what's your mind say to this?" Cathcart asked.

"I wouldn't want to take charity," the boy answered.

"Oh, you'd earn your way, young man," Mrs. Morris insisted. "But you'd get the Christian upbringing your mother would want, and you'd pick up a bit of cash money over room and board. And if your heart's set on running horses or tending cattle next year, there'd be no barred door or rawhide whip to hold you back."

"Well, Rat?" Mitch asked. "Figure you can stand my snorin'?"

"Done it before," Erastus answered. "Truth is, I miss not havin' a brother 'round."

"When would you want to take him?" the sheriff asked.

"This very minute," Mrs. Morris said, rushing over and halfway choking Erastus in her generous arms. "We'll tend him like our own, Sheriff, and see he comes to no ill."

"I don't suppose a boy could expect better, could he, Erastus?"

"No, sir," Erastus agreed.

The sheriff took Erastus back to the kitchen so he could express his thanks and say farewell to Mrs. Cathcart and the children. Erastus did so, getting another motherly hug, a polite curtsy from Becky, and a whispered plea to join the swimming from Busby.

"I'd stay if you wanted, you know," Erastus whispered to the sheriff before turning toward the Morrises.

"You're welcome there, son," Cathcart explained. "It's a good home with plenty o' comforts. You'll get along fine."

"I know I will," Erastus said, gripping the sheriff's hand. He then hurried to join Mitch and the family they would share thereafter.

Chapter Five

After the horrors experienced at the Plank place, anything would have been a welcome change. And in truth the Morrises provided good food and kindly treatment. There was Mitch, too, to swap tales and share wayward thoughts. For the most part those thoughts never got past their amber scalps. Mary Morris ran a taut household, with prayers at mealtime and Bible verses read every night. Erastus had fallen into a world of starched collars and Philadelphia shoes, with little time for anything besides work, lessons, and prayer.

"You're behind on your learning, I'm afraid," Mrs. Morris declared the first time she glimpsed Erastus's pitiful scrawl in her ledgers. "We'll remedy that. I've got Mitchell's old school books set aside, and I'll tend to your ciphers myself."

"A man don't need so much learnin' to run down range ponies," Erastus objected.

"Well, I never heard anyone balk at a chance to better himself, Erastus

Hadley. Here the Lord's handed you a splendid opportunity, and you'd throw it away like a ball of used string."

Erastus bit his lip. He feared telling her how a use could always be found for a bit of string, but reading stories about princes or dragons wouldn't sink a fence post.

Lessons weren't the only vexation to face the boy. He tended the mercantile counter two full hours in the morning and three each afternoon. When there wasn't a customer to help, and that was most of the time, he'd sit atop a hard oak stool and fidget. The monotony of life threatened to drown him!

So it was that Erastus rarely missed the chance to escape with Mitch out to the river and the Brazos hills that would always ring with recollections of his father and mother, of a better life behind. Upon returning, retribution was swift and sure. John Morris knew how to use a belt, and Mary assigned both miscreants extra verses.

"Don't think Pa puts his heart in it, though," Mitch confessed afterward. "He likes to ride himself."

"Yer ma's plumb put out, though," Erastus observed.

"Oh, she thinks boys are the devil's henchmen. Could be she's right, too."

"Could be," Erastus added with a grin.

As summer passed into fall, and winter came and went, Erastus Hadley regained his old spirits. Between the fare provided at the Morris table and tidbits offered by Becky Cathcart or some of the town women, he began to flesh over his bones once more. Bit by bit he grew taller. His shoulders took on muscle, and he lost the gaunt, empty stare Otto Plank had placed in his eyes.

Oh, he was sure to be no giant, for his father had been a smallish man. Most of the town boys had four or five inches on him, and Mitch was half a foot taller. But nobody gave him any trouble, for there was a rock hardness in Rat Hadley, and he could latch hold of an enemy and punish him considerable.

Naturally he wasn't overly fond of being called Rat, but Mitch rarely used anything else, and by now the whole town had settled on it. To make matters worse, the pointed Hadley nose had grown to excess, and even Mary Morris remarked he resembled his rodent namesake.

"You can't help bein' what you are," Mitch declared. "And there are worse names a body could come by."

Rat Hadley wondered.

After a year of tending counter, memorizing Bible verses, and sitting beneath the watchful gaze of Mr. Thadeus Barley in the Thayerville schoolhouse, Rat could hardly contain his joy when Orville Hanks happened by with an invite to help the Circle H roundup crew.

"Got a trail herd to put together, son," the rancher explained. "You and Mitch are welcome to come along, scare in a few strays and help with brandin'. I'll pay you ten silver dollars a week and feed you to boot."

"The boy has chores here, and I need Mitch in the storeroom," Mrs. Morris objected.

"Ma'am, ain't a way under heaven you'll keep them boys to indoor work with 'em sproutin' like July beans. Sometimes you got to give a spry colt its head, you know."

"He's right, dear," Mr. Morris agreed. "Leave them to go. We won't have any business to speak of until harvest anyway. The men will all be heading to Kansas."

"Not my boys!" she argued.

"Not this year anyhow," Hanks replied with a grin. "Give 'em another year and best Dodge City look out."

Mitch was the first to raise a howl, but Rat added his own a second later. Bright and early next morning the two of them rode atop Mitch's speckled mare to the line camp, and thence along to where Orville Hanks was assembling his roundup crew. Every boy in the county was there or else at one of the other ranches, and there were extra men hired on, too. Rat and Mitch rode out with Payne Oakley and Braxton Holley four or five miles upriver. The four of them began driving scattered longhorns out of the tangled ravines and back toward the main camp.

It wasn't easy work. In fact it was near as hard a thing as Rat had ever put his hands to. He choked on dust, drowned in his own sweat, and twice near got the sharp point of a horn for his efforts. Toward twilight he swam in the river with Mitch, and the two of them compared aches and bruises.

"Can't abide that pinto cow pony Payne set me on," Mitch grumbled. "Bites, you know. And the fool critter threw me into a bed o' pencil cactus to boot."

"Your mare's not up to this kind o' work," Rat told his friend. "I got a mustang I'll swap you."

"I seen that one," Mitch said, grinning. "No thanks."

"Ain't any worse'n sittin' on Mr. Barley's oak bench all day!"

"Sure is. I got pains in my bottom that'd unsettle an iron kettle. And at least in the schoolhouse you get to eye Melissa Turnbull."

"Don't you like the view out here?" Rat asked, pointing to the nearby hills.

"Why, all I see's scrub brush and sandstone. Every critter either bites or stings. Don't know why a cowboy takes to such a life."

"Air's good when the cows don't raise any dust, Mitch. And there's Dodge City, too."

"Well, we're not goin' to Kansas, you know."

"Not this year," Rat said, grinning.

As it happened, Rat was already figuring how tall he'd be at sixteen. Even if he didn't grow another inch, though, he vowed to be on his way north next spring. There were excitement and adventures aplenty on the cattle trail, but there was also talk of a railroad coming west from Ft. Worth that would put the trailing days to an end. He didn't plan on missing his chance on account of a year's growth or a few chin whiskers.

Maybe it was that notion that drove him to work so hard. Or perhaps being Rat Hadley he didn't know any other pace. Whatever, Rat was a true wonder on horseback. He outrode most every man in the camp, and his rope rarely missed its mark the first time. As to dogging a calf or running a reluctant bull back to the herd, he had few equals.

"Boy's small and real stringy," Oakley told Orville Hanks. "But I'll tell you right now, Mr. Hanks, I'd take him for a partner any day. He don't quit on a critter, and he's quicker'n a greased pig. The horses treat him like family."

"It's the Hadley blood," Hanks announced. "Can't breed a nag and get a cuttin' pony. You want a cattleman, you got to start with the right stock."

"You hear that, Rat?" Oakley called. "Mr. Hanks says you might just have the makin's."

"I take that as high praise, sir," Rat answered. "Pa always thought you hung the moon, Mr. Hanks."

"I valued your pa, too," Hanks replied. "Won't be long 'fore you're ready to trail steers to market, Rat."

"I'm eager to try, Mr. Hanks. Give me a chance."

"Next year, boy. I got a full crew now, but I'll have a place waitin' next year."

"I'll be here!" Rat shouted, tossing his hat into the air.

That same night while riding guard Rat observed a pair of shadows approaching through a narrow ravine. At first he thought they might be boys come to visit their fathers or maybe somebody coming back from a late swim. Their bare shoulders and thin frames made it seem likely. But as they came closer, the faint moonlight illuminated them, and Rat saw they were wearing buckskin leggings and carrying bows.

"Comanches," he whispered. He then turned his horse away from them and hurried to wake Payne Oakley.

"How many?" the ranch foreman asked when Rat jabbered his alarm.

"I saw two, but there could be more."

"Well, I'll get the boss. Then we'll have a look."

"They could have half the herd run off by then," Rat warned. "Don't you think we ought to fire a couple o' shots, wake the boys?"

"You want to spend all summer gettin' this herd back together?" Oakley cried. "No, leave the cows to their peace, Rat. We'll have a look see."

So it was that Oakley roused Orville Hanks, and the two men followed Rat to where he'd spotted the Indians. The Comanches had vanished, but they'd left a moccasin trail. Rat picked it up easily and threaded his way down the ravine and along to the river. A small band of haggard Indians roasted slices of a slain longhorn over a campfire.

"Want me to fetch the others?" Rat asked when Hanks and Oakley joined him.

"No, they're about done for, those Indians," Hanks observed. "Leave 'em to what days are left to 'em. Look good, Rat. Won't be too much longer you see Indians off a reservation."

"No, sir," Rat whispered.

"You go along back to the herd now, son. Payne and I'll see nothin' comes o' this."

Rat nodded and headed back. He recalled his pa's terrifying tales of murderous Comanches. It seemed the wild had been worked out of them now. Others than Otto Plank had a whip, he supposed.

It wasn't but a few days later that the last calf was branded, and the trail crew took charge of the herd. Even as the mass of men and beeves turned northward, those left behind prepared to return home.

"You did a fine job, boy," Hanks said as he paid off each of the roundup boys in turn. Besides the promised silver, Hanks had generously doled out a horse to each hand.

"Wouldn't want a cowboy walkin' home, would I, Rat?" he asked when he handed the boy his wages, plus a twenty-dollar gold piece as a sort of bonus. "You write your mother I send my respects, too."

"Yessir," Rat said, thinking of how his last letter was written just after Christmas. He'd gotten three from Austin since then.

"And get some growth on you," Hanks added. "Texas needs its Hadleys tall and rangy."

"Never knew 'em to come that way," Rat answered with a grin and a nod of thanks. "But we do our best anyway."

"That's a truth, son. You write that letter now. I expect you've neglected it long enough."

"Afraid it's true," Rat confessed, gazing at his feet. "I promise to get after it, though."

"See you do. And don't run all the rough off that mustang. Man needs a horse that'll take him places."

"Yes, sir," Rat agreed as the cattleman turned to leave. But there wasn't really any place to ride.

Just the same Rat wasn't in any mood to head back to Thayerville just yet, and he found Mitch equally reluctant. The two of them wandered along the river until they spied a low hill topped by the grandfather of all white oaks. There wasn't a bigger tree for twenty miles, and the boys were drawn to it like iron shavings to a magnet.

"I remember this tree," Rat remarked. "Pa brought me up here once. We dug arrowheads out o' the river, and Pa said it must've been an old Indian campin' spot."

"You sure?" Mitch asked.

"Shoot, Mitch, ain't no mistakin' that tree. She's a giant."

"What's that there, Rat? Over to the rocks."

Rat turned his horse and made his way cautiously past a pile of boulders and along to where someone had planted a wagon plank in the hard ground.

"It's a grave," Rat said, sliding off his horse and gazing at the words scratched in the plank.

HEER LYS TOM BOSWELL
HOO WAS LONG ON HORS CINTS
BUT SHORT ON LUK

"Likely he was a cowboy," Mitch said solemnly.

"More'n likely kilt trailin' cows last summer," Rat added. "Lots o' outfits cross the river hereabouts. Could be he got thrown. Or snake bit. Lots o' cottonmouths along here."

"Could be. Poor luck, bein' kilt just settin' out."

"Might've been halfway if he came up from way south o' San Antonio."

"Not to Dodge City yet, though. All those miles just to drown or get bit."

"Some men don't have much luck, Mitch."

"Or none at all," Mitch said, shaking his head sadly. "Me, I got some. I still got Ma and Pa, and I don't go to bed hungry. Still, it ain't exactly lively 'round our place."

"It's paradise compared to some places," Rat declared, thinking of the Plank farm three miles south of the river.

"You figure you got luck, Rat?"

"Oh, yeah, lots o' it. All hard. Truth is, if it wasn't for hard luck, I'd not have a drop o' it."

"It was good luck the sheriff fetched you from ole man Plank's farm."

"No, I figure that was you," Rat declared. "Maybe you bein' my friend's good luck, though."

"You might've done better if I was one o' the Hanks boys."

"Oh, they got no time for the likes o' me, Mitch. Nobody much does. Rat Hadley ain't anything for folks to pay mind to. Most don't, you know."

"Don't sell yourself so short. I know Mr. Hanks won't be settin' any praise on my horsemanship. Shoot, he give you a twenty-dollar bonus, too."

"Most likely that was from feelin' guilty 'bout sendin' us packin' after Pa got kilt."

"He promised to take you north next year."

"Well, guess I'll have to see that 'fore I take it to heart more'n a little. It's a long time till next spring, and lots o' things can happen."

"Won't any o' them happen as we stand 'round here gazin' at that grave. How 'bout tryin' your hand at landin' a big Brazos catfish for supper?"

"Cut some limbs," Rat answered. "I'll tend the horses."

"Tie 'em good, Rat. Heard there were Comanches hereabouts."

"They got too good an eye for horseflesh to bother with yer mare, Mitch. Nor with this scraggly excuse for a mustang o' mine, neither. Now get along to work and we'll have time to swim some. It's more'n middlin' warm today."

"Hot 'nough to fry bacon on the rocks," Mitch muttered. "Likely the

Lord's givin' us a taste o' what Ma's sure to preach us on when we get home."

"Could be," Rat said, laughing at the notion. "Or how our bottoms'll feel if yer pa cuts a switch."

Mitch laughed along for a minute as he cut fishing poles with an over-sized knife. Later, after Rat satisfied himself the horses had good grass, the boys dipped lines in the river and managed to snag a trio of fat river cats for their dinner. Then they splashed away the balance of the afternoon in the river before frying up the fish.

"Never knew the night to be so quiet," Mitch said as they spread their blankets on either side of the dying embers.

"Oh, it's mostly quiet," Rat explained. "Gives a man chance to do some thinkin'. So Pa used to tell me."

"Think 'bout what?"

"Anything. Everything."

"And what you thinkin' on just now?"

"Poor ole Boswell over there and his bad luck. Wonder what it feels like, dyin' so young," Rat mumbled. " 'Course, I suppose he might've been older."

"Older'n us maybe," Mitch admitted. "But I'd guess he was young all the same. Elsewise they wouldn't't've thought it so ill luck o' him to mark his board the way they did."

"Sure, you're likely right."

"Rat, I worry 'bout dyin' sometimes. It worries me."

"Not me. Ain't no more hurtin' when yer gone."

"No more anything. And that scares me plenty."

"Yeah, it does unsettle you some."

Chapter Six

There were other nights spent along the river those next two years—interludes of adventure and distraction from a world of long, tedious days and stifling nights at the Morris place in Thayerville. A disappointed Rat Hadley listened soberly when Orville Hanks explained how sour cattle prices forced him to trim his trail crew and leave boys of sixteen behind.

"I'd go 'long for the adventure o' it," Rat had pleaded.

"Only 'cause you never tasted trail dust, son," Hanks had answered. "Learn this much. Never do a job without demandin' all that's due you, Rat. Folks don't respect a man doesn't call for his wages. There'll be another year for Kansas."

So there was, but it sometimes seemed to Rat it was an eternity coming.

Rat could hardly conceal his excitement the day Payne Oakley strode into the mercantile with an invitation to join the Hanks roundup crew again.

"The boy's got duties here," Mrs. Morris argued as she stepped between Rat and the veteran cowboy. "You haul him off, he and Mitch the both of them every spring, and I'm left with nobody to tend counter until you finish with them."

"Ma'am, I know it's a hardship," Oakley confessed, "but this town and this county eats off the money we collect at Dodge City. Can't be a trail herd without boys to scare up strays."

"What about afterwards?" Rat asked. "Any chance o' signin' on for the ride north?"

"That'd be Mr. Hanks's say so," Oakley answered, "but I'd judge you've earned your spurs. Little more o' you than last year, too. Could just be you'll measure up to what's taken for a Texas cowboy along the Brazos."

Rat grinned as he discarded his apron and carefully closed out the daily totals in Mrs. Morris's ledger. Then he gave the woman a faint smile.

"That's no kind o' farewell," Oakley barked, and the boy trotted over and gave Mrs. Morris a warm hug.

"I'll not likely keep a job open for you," she warned with a softening frown.

"No, ma'am. Wouldn't expect it," Rat told her. "I never was a man to tend counter all his days, though. I belong out on the range atop some shaggy ole mustang."

"Once," she admitted. "But you've developed a fair hand, and you're quick with the figures. I'd take you for a banker if I didn't know better."

"Thanks, ma'am," Rat said, sweeping a wayward hank of hair off his forehead. "I'll be back to see you 'fore headin' north. I promise you that."

"I suppose Mitch is sure to want to go, too," she grumbled. "Well, you've got time to pack up some things. Get yourself a fresh shirt and an extra pair of trousers. You wear out the seats of them faster than anybody I ever saw. I'll pack you up some food, too. No trail cook ever fed a boy enough to keep him from starving."

"Guess I'll be a while," Rat told Oakley. "I'll fetch Mitch along with me. We'll be in 'fore dark."

"Take your time. No hurry, Rat. Long as you're ready to chase cows tomorrow at dawn."

"Yessir," Rat said, grinning at the thought.

Once Mary Morris had satisfied herself the boys had all that was needed for their stint in the roundup camp, Rat summoned Mitch from the storeroom, and the two friends hurried down to the livery to get their horses. Once mounted, they returned to the mercantile so Mitch could make his farewells, and soon they were racing each other north to the river and to the Hanks place. They arrived to a mixture of taunts and cheers, for the cowboys had heard all about Rat's extended good-bye.

"Sure you don't want to bring Ma along, sonny?" a lanky South Texan named Bob Tripp asked.

"She's too old for you, Bob," Oakley cried. "And married to boot."

"Don't take 'em old," Tripp said, shaking his head as the other men hooted. "As to married, well . . ."

It was good that Rat Hadley began that arduous week and a half of roundup with a grin, for there were few to follow. Most days he was too weary to share an evening swim with Mitch down by where the river flowed past unlucky Tom Boswell's grave. Roundup was a world of dust and sweat and blood—more exhaustion than adventure. And where before men seemed to enjoy a boy's company, they now expected a man's labors.

"They're testin' us," Mitch observed as the two of them shared night watch. "Seein' if we're up to goin' north."

"I am," Rat declared. "But my backside's nary so sure."

Mitch laughed. "Do better if you didn't go draggin' it through every bed o' cactus in tarnation. Cain't you stay atop a horse nowadays?"

Mitch was referring to Rat's efforts at breaking in a pair of range ponies. There was a fearful lot of learning due before Rat Hadley would pass for anybody's notion of a bronc buster!

"I didn't notice you takin' a hand at it," Rat growled. "And wasn't it you roped the corral yesterday chasin' that heifer to the branders?"

"Yeah, that was me," Mitch said, hiding his red face. "I'm not much of a cowboy. But then it's not me has to prove himself."

"Eh?"

"I figure if the old man takes you, he'll ask me. And I'd judge he wouldn't leave you back again. Not with you sproutin' chin whiskers and growin' out o' yer trousers."

"Ain't size makes a cowboy," Rat said, sitting up straighter so that the four inches he was shy of Mitch wouldn't seem so much. "It's what he can do on a horse. And I'll put myself up against the best in the outfit."

" 'Specially at collectin' cactus spines," Mitch said, laughing.

Rat continued to put his all into the roundup. Each time he saw Orville Hanks, the boy spoke of the trail drive and hinted at his eagerness to join the outfit.

"Yessir, be a fine chance for a man," Rat remarked. Hanks nodded, but offered nothing further.

Finally the roundup came to an end. The trail herd grazed beside the river, and the younger boys rolled their possessions into their blankets and prepared to set off homeward. Hanks paid them off one by one. Rat and Mitch stood to one side, nervously dreading the moment when their own names might be called.

"Rat Hadley," Hanks called, and there was a murmur of complaint among the cowboys. "Rat?"

"Here, Mr. Hanks," Rat said, stumbling forward with bowed head.

"Figured you made the trail crew, did you?" Hanks asked.

"We all thought he did!" Bob Tripp shouted.

"Well, I never took a boy to Kansas with toes stickin' out o' his boots," Hanks explained. "And that poor excuse for a hat you got wouldn't keep cloud spit off your face. Try this out."

Payne Oakley stepped forward with a broad-brimmed gray hat fresh off a store shelf, and Hanks himself offered a pair of polished black boots, with spurs securely attached.

"Don't know what to say," Rat mumbled.

"The boots come from me," Hanks explained. "Hat's from the boys. We got one somewhere for Mitch, too. You'll the both o' you need 'em where we're headed."

"Dodge City?" Mitch cried.

"And the devil's own country 'tween here and there," Hanks announced. "Get along to town and say your good-byes. We leave at dawn."

"Yessir!" Rat yelled, tossing his old hat aside and pulling the new one down over his ears. "Thank you all, fellows. Mitch and I won't be lettin' you down."

"Sure won't," Oakley barked. "We'll see to that."

And so Rat Hadley and Mitch Morris finally set off northward toward Dodge City along the overgrazed and wagon rutted Western Cattle Trail. Not so long ago wild Indians raided herds beyond the Brazos, and renegade whites prowled the empty country north of the Trinity and south of Red River Station. Eighteen-eighty was on the horizon now, though, and what

Indians a cowboy saw were mostly toll collectors in the Nations or strays come to beg a steer or two.

Nature hadn't had the wild worked out of her, though, and peril aplenty remained. The outfit fought back a stampede just north of the Trinity, and the Red River crossing was mired in quicksand. Ten steers were lost to the bog, and three others broke legs and merited shooting. The sole solace was a fair feast afterward.

"I feel like I've been mashed like a potato," Mitch muttered as he collapsed in his blankets that night. "Never ate so much dust in my whole life, and then they near drowned me today! If I never see another cow it'll be too soon."

"You wanted to come," Rat reminded his friend. "Me, even if I ate drag dust a lifetime, I'd rather be out here'n back o' yer ma's counter. Long as there's stars up there to look at, and good company nearby, I got no complaints."

Shortly thunderheads rolled in, swallowing the stars. Mitch only grinned.

It was up near the Cimarron crossing that real trouble found the Circle H. Just shy of the river three dust-covered riders appeared near the left flank. As they swung along the fringe of the herd to where Rat struggled in the dusty wake, one of them made a move to cut out a few steers.

Ain't much a man can do 'bout it, Rat told himself as he turned his horse to the right and galloped to fetch Payne Oakley. Orville Hanks forbid his men to shoot off handguns for fear of stampedes, and a bullet was the best reply to attempted thievery. There were a handful of armed riders, though—experienced hands like Oakley. When Rat reached the foreman, Oakley nodded his understanding of the muddled alarm.

"Don't you worry for now, Rat," Oakley replied. "It's an old trick, just a way to draw off the crew while raiders hit elsewhere. We'll bring in the strays tonight."

"And for now?"

"Nudge the herd a little harder. We'll be on the near bank o' the river this afternoon. That's when they'll hit."

"You sure?"

"Been up this way before, son. There's three, four outfits prowl the Cimarron country, and not a one of 'em's ever snatched a Circle H beef and not paid a price."

Rat nodded although he had no idea of what lay ahead.

It was Bob Tripp began pulling in riders from the fringes. He handed others pistols or rifles. The best guns went into the steadiest hands. Tripp led Rat and Mitch to a narrow slit of a ravine crowning a low hill near the river.

"It's a cowboy fort o' sorts," Tripp explained. "I expect the first to fight here shot it out with Comanches. We got a different sort o' varmint to tend."

"Rustlers?" Mitch asked nervously.

"Oh, a rustler comes by dead o' night, swipes a few head off the range. These fellows travel in small armies, and they take a whole herd."

"And the cowboys?" Rat asked.

"Shoot the varmints full o' lead or else get peppered 'emselves. Now you boys pay attention. I got a pair o' Colts for you. They'll kick you to Missouri, but they kill sure and quick. Trick's to hold 'em steady—with both your hands. Don't go tryin' to spit fire like a circus clown. Aim, hold her straight, and squeeze off each shot. You got to double click the hammer, you know. Do it with your right thumb. Then all you do's pull the old trigger. And be ready for the kick. It'll throw you some the first few times."

"I never shot at a man before," Rat confessed. "Never even thought on it."

"Me neither," Mitch confessed.

"Ain't men you're shootin' at now," Tripp barked. "Varmints wearin' pants. Ain't so important you hit anybody, you know. Just that you make 'em know you're up here ready to."

Tripp then turned to go, and Rat called out anxiously.

"Ain't no boy ever signed on to trail beeves," Tripp howled angrily. "I showed you what I could. Now I got to go look after the other ones."

Rat nodded. As Tripp rode back to the herd, the boys fingered the cold steel of the pistols and stared off across the flat, ravine-scarred land. Was there ever so empty a place? And Rat thought back to that little hill above the Brazos and the lonely grave of Tom Boswell.

"It's Boswell's luck we're havin'," he sighed. Mitch grinned sourly, then nodded.

The raiders came as promised. Their first strike was against the herd itself, but a half dozen cowboys poured a hot fire on them, and they bounced off and charged the hill instead. As Rat waited for the first outlaw to get within range, he counted the horsemen. There were ten, eleven, twelve of them. The lead man wore a great sprawling moustache. Rat motioned for Mitch to take him. Rat himself drew a bead on the second rider, a fresh-faced boy no older than himself. The horsemen hurled themselves closer, but they had to slow to ascend the hill. Then, as they got to within fifty feet of the ravine, Rat cocked his Colt and fired. The pistol exploded, numbing his fingers and showering the air with a dark powder cloud. Mitch shot, too. The young men blinked the stinging powder from their eyes and fired again. And again. They had no inkling as to the accuracy of their shooting. It was the noise and the powder smoke more than anything that surprised the raiders and flung them back.

"I think I got one o' them," Mitch shouted excitedly as he stared at a lump frozen on the slope below. "Or you did."

"Look there," Rat cried as Bob Tripp led seven vengeful cowboys after the confused bandits. Again the raiders made a move toward the hill, but they soon vanished in a swirl of smoke and fire. When it was all over a pair of riders managed to flee down the Cimarron. The others clutched bleeding arms or bellies. Or lay in the dust where they'd fallen.

"You did just fine," Tripp declared afterward as he joined the shaken novices. "Held 'em at bay, let us close in from behind."

"Was a close thing," Rat said, popping open the cylinder of his Colt. "I only had one bullet left."

"I shot all six o' mine," Mitch added.

"Bob Tripp, you're an addled fool!" Tripp cried. "You forgot to give 'em shells. Lord, I'm sorry, boys. Could've got you kilt."

"Wouldn't've been time to reload anyhow," Rat muttered. "Any o' our people hurt?"

"Bert Cobble's dead. Luke Granger's close to. Took a pair o' bullets in his side. Payne's got a shattered wrist."

"And the outlaws?" Mitch inquired.

Tripp waved them along down the hill. Four wounded raiders lay moaning under the barrels of Winchesters. Five corpses lay elbow to elbow nearby, their grizzled faces drained of life. The sole remaining body lay as it had fallen on the hillside. Rat stared down at a pair of huge, empty blue eyes frozen on a fuzz-faced youth.

"Was the one you took," Mitch said, nervously slapping Rat on the back. "Look at it, Bob. One bullet through the cheek."

"Cain't be older'n me," Rat said, shivering with a sudden chill.

"Old as he'll get," Tripp noted. "Give me a hand. We'll drag him down with the others."

Rat grabbed a still-warm hand while Mitch took the other. Tripp lifted the feet. It was a light load for three men, no effort at all. And as they laid it beside the others, Rat silently prayed for forgiveness.

"Can't blame yourself, Rat," Mitch said, reading his friend's thoughts. "Shoot, if Tripp hadn't come 'long when he did, could be us over there."

"Don't make it easier, Mitch. Did you see him? Could've been Alex."

"Wasn't. Don't you see, Rat? It's just like ole Boswell. No luck, that boy. Fell upon bad company, and got a bullet for his mistake. Now come along. I got a need to wash all this powder and dust off me 'fore the cows muddy up the river."

Rat readily agreed. It wasn't just powder and dust he was freeing himself from, though. There was a need to shed the shadowy grip of cold death. By the time he finally climbed out of the river and returned to the outfit, all traces of the raiders had been erased. A single mound of earth topped by rocks marked their grave. There wasn't a sign of the wounded, and Rat didn't ask after them. Payne Oakley, one arm in a sling, sipped whiskey from a hitherto hidden flask, and the other veterans seemed more than usually grim. Rat took their dead eyes for an answer.

After crossing the Cimarron, it was relatively easy to hurry the cattle along to Dodge City on the Arkansas. The town was little more than sprawling cattle pens, railroad tracks, and a hodgepodge of plaı gambling houses and saloons. Rat accepted his wages and thanked Orville Hanks for the chance to prove himself. Then he followed Mitch down the street in search of a bathhouse.

Trail's end was as wild an event as any tale had hinted, and Rat soon found himself caught up in the celebration. Three other Texas outfits were in Dodge City, and sixty cowboys could raise a roof or two. After bathing in perfumed suds and making a stop at the barber for a clipping and shave, the boys headed for Front Street, decked out in fresh clothes and looking fit for a parson's visit. In no time they exchanged a few silver coins for a bottle, and the fiery swirl of whiskey surged through them.

"Well, here's some fresh blood!" a tall, willowy girl declared as she draped a boa over Mitch's arm. "Care to dance, Texas?"

"Yes, ma'am," Mitch replied, abandoning the bottle and Rat for the attentions of the female.

"How 'bout you, sonny?" a woman in her mid-twenties asked, approaching Rat. "Got some dancin' in you?"

"Never tried," Rat said, dropping his gaze as the woman came closer. The front of her dress cut down into her belly, leaving little to the imagination. Rat managed to grin shyly as she took his hand.

"Go 'head, Rat!" Bob Tripp urged.

Rat scowled, but the woman only grinned. "Rat?" she asked. "Well, he do look a bit like one."

"It's 'cause my name's Erastus," Rat told her, angrily scanning the room.

"Well, Erastus, you look peaked. Don't you worry 'bout it. Bit o' lovin's sure to cure that. Let Flora take you somewhere quiet where we can get to know each other."

"Set the price early, kid," a cowboy cried, laughing.

"Let go," Rat said, wriggling free. He stared at the amused faces of the encircling men, wanting to strike out at each and every one of them. Finally he swallowed his anger and stormed outside.

Mitch found him three hours later tossing stones into the Arkansas River.

"Rat?" he called.

"Who am I to be laughed at so?" Rat howled. "Is it always goin' to be this way?"

"Was only in fun," Mitch argued. "And it'll pass."

"Will it?" Rat asked. He wondered.

Chapter Seven

Most of the veteran cowboys blew off a little steam, bought themselves an outfit or two, and drifted slowly southward. Mitch Morris, on the other hand, developed a talent at the card tables. From early afternoon to well after midnight the seventeen-year-old would test his wits against older, more experienced players. There were some true artists in Dodge City that summer, but even shaved cards and extra aces didn't deter Mitch. He won more than he lost, so he stayed on.

Rat Hadley found no like success in Dodge. He had a good mind for figures, and the plain truth was that you couldn't win at cards. It was clear to see! Hard liquor left him wheezing and bewildered, and the girls spent most of their time picking at his name or making fun of his manners. All in all, he'd been happier elsewhere.

"I've had my fill o' Kansas," Rat finally told Mitch. "I got a bit o' money left, and nobody's stabbed or shot me yet. So I'd judge I'm well off by Dodge City standards and ready to ride south."

Mitch put it simply. "I'm not," he declared. "May never be. The cards keep comin' my way, I might just become a professional. Mighty easy life, Rat. I could use a friend to watch my back, though. Many's the card-sharp paid somebody to peek at another player's hand."

"I'm not the one for that kind o' work," Rat argued. "I close to cough myself sick from the cigar smoke, and I miss Texas. Haven't had a swim since Cimarron River, and yer ma's certain to worry after us."

"We'll write her a letter. Tell her we've started up a business."

"No, you write the letter, Mitch. I'll deliver it personal."

"Won't hold it against me, my stayin' on?"

"Couldn't ever do that," Rat said, shaking his head at Mitch's easy smile. "You ain't no cowboy, Mitch. Never'll make a livin' ropin' steers or roundin' up strays. Me, I'm out o' place in a town. Guess I belong with the horses."

"Don't sell yourself short."

"That's for other folks to do," Rat replied. "Me, I don't fool myself either way. Ain't much to look on, and a runt to boot, but I'll work hard for the man that pays me. And I remember my friends."

"Am I one o' them?"

"Top o' the list, Mitch. You saved my life. Be a hard thing to forget."

"Good thing to know, that," Mitch said, sighing. "A body has needs o' friends."

On his way back to Texas Rat Hadley learned the truth of those words. Crossing the wild Cimarron country he was shot at two times and chased a third. It was a fine game, separating Texas cowboys from their earnings, and many a desperado tried his hand at it. Rat quickly regretted hanging around Dodge City so long. How much better it would have been to return with Payne Oakley and Orville Hanks!

As it turned out Rat felt safest riding among the Indian camps and reservations farther south. Once, among the Caddos, he was treated to fresh trout and corn bread. The Choctaws fed him, too, but for a price. They, after all, were Americanized.

Once across the Red River, nothing short of a full-blown cyclone could keep him from Thayerville. He rode forty miles some days, and he forded rivers with less concern than a man stepped across a mud puddle. When he got to the Brazos, he paused beside the white oak and washed the dust and weariness from himself and his clothes. He walked past old Boswell's grave, but wind or vandals had carried off the board, and time had evened out the ground so you couldn't tell anybody had ever been buried there.

"Well, time passes," Rat whispered to the wind. "Nobody lasts for long alive, so I guess you cain't expect to do better dead."

He rode into Thayerville early the next morning. All the way from Kansas he'd been rehearsing the words he'd share with Mary Morris. But when he stepped inside the mercantile, he was unprepared for what he found. Sitting behind the counter was a pleasant-faced boy of fifteen or so, and a second youngster maybe a year younger restocked shelves.

"Mornin'," the stockboy called as Rat stared at the counter—*his* counter. "What can I get you, mister?"

"I'm Rat Hadley," the newcomer explained.

"Josh Morris," the youngest boy answered, offering his hand. "Yonder's my brother Jeremiah. We just come out from Tyler to help our aunt."

"Miz Morris handy?" Rat asked.

"I'll fetch her," Josh said, hurrying toward the storeroom. Moments later he reappeared with Mary Morris.

"Mornin', ma'am," Rat said.

"Lord be praised," Mrs. Morris cried, rushing over and wrapping Rat up in her arms. She kissed and hugged and close to squeezed him silly. Finally she let go and asked about Mitch.

"He stayed in Dodge City," Rat explained, handing her Mitch's letter.

"Doing what?" Mrs. Morris asked.

"Well, he found himself a job o' sorts," Rat said, praying he wouldn't give out too much of the truth. Mary Morris deemed cards the devil's own tools, and she condemned them mightily.

"Well, he's of an age to find distractions," she muttered. "Knew it when you left. If a boy sees too much of the country, he's never content around home. I wrote my sister-in-law, and she sent her two eldest up to help with the store."

"For the summer?" Rat asked.

"No, they'll stay on till they finish their schooling. Unless they run off on some fool cattle drive."

"Angry with me 'bout that, ma'am?"

"No, I couldn't get very angry at you, Rat," she confessed. "And the range has done you good. You've grown, and your color's better.

Knowing your father, I don't suppose settled life ever would take with you."

"Probably not," he agreed. "Still, I thought maybe you might could use me at the store a bit."

"Lord, Rat, I've brought the boys down to tend counter. Gave them the upstairs room, too. I thought now you were working for Mr. Hanks you wouldn't want to come back."

"Well, I can't blame you for it ma'am. Guess I should've spoken with you. Mr. Hanks, he's got his regular crew, you see. He might could put me on just the same."

"I'm certain he will. Mitch says you outride any other man in the county. If tending cows is what you want to do with your life, it's best you got along with it."

"Yes, ma'am."

And so, after sharing a bite of lunch with the Morrises and spinning tales of the cattle drive, Rat remounted his horse and headed out to visit the county's ranches. He met with poor results.

"Glad you made it home, son," Mr. Hanks said, "but you know I've got a full crew."

"I thought maybe since Payne's arm . . ."

"It's healed just fine, Rat. I might need a man this winter, but for now I've nothin'. I didn't get my price in Dodge, you know. Truth is I'm lettin' men go, not takin' any on."

"Yessir," Rat said, nodding sadly as he turned to go.

It was much the same up and down the Brazos. Falling prices meant tightening belts. People would feed him in return for a bit of wood chopping, and a woman paid him to mend a fence and repair her pump. Down on the Colorado he helped raise a barn, and in Wood City the town doctor kept Rat busy painting a house.

Rat was at it day and night for two weeks, slapping whitewash on the bare planks as the fiery August sun blazed down on his bare shoulders. The doctor's daughter often watched from the porch and sometimes brought Rat a ladle of spring water.

"Thanks, miss," Rat always replied.

"You're quite welcome, Rat," she answered, smiling shyly. "Do you mind my asking how a pleasant boy like yourself could come across such a name?"

"Well, it ain't my name really," Rat confessed. "Comes o' my given name, Erastus. I never took to it really, but people went on callin' me that, and I couldn't fight all o' them. So I give up and took it on."

"I like Erastus better. It's interesting. Sounds a bit like a banker, or maybe a preacher."

"Wouldn't do for me then," Rat said, laughing. "That'd be one shot fell wide o' the mark."

"I'm called Amanda," she explained. "What do you think of that for a name?"

"Suits you well enough, miss. It's a pretty name, kind o' like a flower. Yeah, it suits you."

She blushed as he returned the ladle. Then he resumed his work, leaving her to watch from afar.

She brought water quite often thereafter, and twice they watched the sunset as he cleaned his brushes.

"Erastus, do you mind me asking a question?" she asked as twilight settled in around them.

"No, Miss Amanda," he told her. "May not be able to answer you, but I'll give her a try."

"It's about those marks on your back," she explained. "Thin scars. I've only seen their kind once in my life. We had a Negro working for us. He'd been horsewhipped while a slave down in Louisiana."

"I don't much like to talk 'bout 'em," Rat mumbled.

"You were whipped, weren't you? As a child."

"Was no child," Rat argued. "Fourteen. Just after my pa passed on, I went to work for a fellow. He was rough with his own boys, and he beat the all o' us regular. Nigh kilt me. Lord was lookin' out for me, I guess. Sheriff rode down and took me away."

"You've had some hard days, haven't you?" she asked, placing her hands on his sweat-streaked shoulders. "It's all written on your face. I wince at the sight of you slaving away in the bright sun, melting away before my eyes. It hurts to see you suffer."

"Oh, I'm used to the heat, miss," Rat said, grinning. "Don't you worry over that."

"I do worry," she insisted, slipping her hands behind his head and pressing herself against him. Bewildered, Rat gazed into her eyes. They were filling up with tears.

"Ma'am, I best go," he said, wriggling free. "I don't think yer pa'd . . ."

"Little late to be thinking of that!" the doctor shouted, rushing to his daughter's side and jerking her away from Rat. "Are you crazed or just plain stupid, boy?"

"Don't know I'm either," Rat barked in reply. "Miss Amanda asked if she could watch the sun go down with me, and I didn't see as how I could say no. I don't own the sun, nor the land under my feet, neither one."

"Don't you fence words with me, young man. Look at you! Standing there half naked, making indecent advances on my daughter!"

"Sir, I done nothin' o' the kind," Rat objected. "I only been paintin' yer house."

"Well, you'll do no more painting here, nor elsewhere in Wood City after I pass word of your attack on my daughter. It may well be you'll feel the bite of a rope before morning."

"Sir, I never . . ."

"We'll settle with him, Pa," a fresh voice called. Before Rat quite knew what was happening, a slender man in his early twenties appeared, accompanied by two boys in their late teens. One tossed a loop over Rat's shoulders, and the others quickly saw to it the painter was bound securely. Then they started on him.

"Papa, no!" Amanda pleaded. "He didn't do anything. I just spoke with him a few times. That's all."

The doctor urged his sons on. Boots followed fists, and Rat dropped to his knees, a shuddering bundle of bruises and pain.

"Lowlife!" they called him. "Gutter trash!"

"Now listen to me!" the doctor said, grabbing Rat by his forelock and lifting his head. "What do you have to say for yourself now?"

"Nothin'," Rat said through a mouthful of blood. "I done nothin'."

"Shall I give you back to the boys?"

"Do what you want," Rat growled. "I done you no harm. If you want to beat me, go ahead. I been beat worse'n you could manage."

"Don't be so sure about that," one of the brothers cried.

Rat only laughed and waited for another blow. He was tired, his ribs ached, and he didn't care anymore. He thought back to that outlaw boy shot on the Cimarron and wondered who'd been the lucky one that day.

"I don't ever want to see your face in Wood City again," the doctor declared, glaring at Rat's swollen face. "Understand?"

"Understand?" Rat asked. "Not a bit o' it. You hire me to do a job o' work, and 'cause yer daughter brings me a dipper o' water or looks at the sun go down, you figure you got the right to beat me silly. Nobody's got that right!"

"Listen to me, trash," the doctor roared. "I might hire a Negro or a Mexican to paint my house, but I wouldn't have either one of them to Sunday supper. Nor tolerate them touching my daughter!"

"Git!" the oldest brother yelled as he pried the ropes from Rat's battered chest. "Don't ever come back, either."

"I'm due wages," Rat complained as he struggled to his feet. One side was turning deep purple, and he thought it likely a rib or two was busted.

"You're due a hangman's noose if I see you here in one hour," the doctor vowed. "Get his horse, Benjamin. Tie him on if you have to, but get him from my sight."

"Sure, Pa," the youngest boy agreed.

"I'll get my own horse," Rat muttered, grabbing a tin of paint and hurling it at the doctor. "The Lord knows yer work this night. I hope to hell he calls you to 'counts."

With that spoken, Rat stumbled to where his horse was tied. He slipped a shirt onto his back and pulled himself into the saddle. He was half of a mind to dig the old Colt Bob Tripp had given him at the Cimarron from the saddlebag and avenge himself on that doctor. But that would only get him hung, and Rat Hadley wasn't ready to die just yet. No, there were things he hadn't done.

He slapped the horse into motion, and the mustang carried him from Wood City and along the Colorado two or three miles. He didn't recall how exactly because his eyes were closed most of that time, and pain enveloped memory. He came to in a narrow barred cell in the jail house of a town called Rosstown. A frowning sheriff met his awakening gaze.

"Just who exactly would you be?" the lawman asked. "You must've done somethin' fine to take such a beatin'. Well?"

Rat stared at his bandaged ribs and tried to manage a reply. Finally he related his tale of the Wood City doctor and of the hard times since leaving Kansas.

"Yeah, the cattle market's gone south for certain," the sheriff agreed. "Didn't figure you was any desperado. No poster with your likeness, and who goes lookin' for trouble with an empty pistol in his saddlebag."

"Never did get me any bullets," Rat said, chuckling.

"Ain't too bright, are you, boy?"

"Don't seem so," Rat confessed. "I been to a school to learn readin' and writin', and I know how to ride and tend cows. But I got no knack with people at all. Far as human critters go, I'm dumber'n spit."

"Well, many a man could say that," the sheriff declared as he unlocked the cell. "Don't know a man can get himself locked up on account o' it, though. Best take it easy on them ribs awhile. One's cracked, I'm guessin'."

"I free to go?" Rat asked.

"Long as you stay out o' trouble. Got a home, boy?"

"Not to speak of," Rat confessed.

"Where you come from?"

"All over. Nowhere. Guess you'd say Thayerville. I lived there a time."

"Then my advice'd be to go back. Folks what know you'll give you a better chance. A boy like you rangin' about's certain to find bad fortune."

"It's 'bout all the fortune I ever come by."

"Well, things can change, youngster. Seen it before. Your horse is over to the livery. Tell Hi Garner I told him the oats and water's on the county."

"I got some money," Rat objected.

"You may need it elsewhere. Now get along 'fore I change my mind. And may God look after you. Sure somebody best do it."

Chapter Eight

Rat Hadley was two years getting back to Thayerville. He passed six months on a Hood County ranch, then made the long drive north to Kansas once again. He wandered to Colorado afterward, and thence across the Llano, doing this and that. Nothing lasted long, though, and with worsening cattle markets, ranch work wasn't to be had. He rounded up a string of range ponies only to find no buyers. Under a hot August sun he followed the shiny rails of the new Texas and Pacific railroad to Weatherford before riding north to Thayerville.

The town had done some changing. A half dozen houses spread out along the Weatherford market road, and a brick bank now dominated the center of Main Street. There were two saloons now, a small café, and a new Methodist church alongside the old schoolhouse. Rat shuddered a moment as he rode past the Morris place. Someone had added a false brick front and turned it into a hotel. Down the street, though, a new and larger mercantile stood near the livery.

"Two years," Rat murmured as he traced the thin brownish growth on his upper lip. It could almost pass for a moustache. Even as he was wondering whether anyone would recognize him, a voice called out from the street.

"Rat!"

Rat turned and gazed upon a youngish man in a banker's suit, complete with string tie and bowler hat, waving from the door of the hotel.

"Mitch?"

Mitchell Morris trotted out into the dusty street, and Rat swung himself off his horse to greet his old friend. The two of them locked wrists, grinning and nodding and babbling too fast to be understood.

"Seen Ma and Pa?" Mitch finally managed.

"Seen nobody," Rat answered. "Just got in."

"Well, we best see to it right off. She'd hide the both o' us for keepin' you a secret. Lord, it's been a while. You went and got some growth."

Rat nodded. He was still a good four inches shy of six feet, but it was as tall as he was likely to get. Hadley men ran to small, it seemed. When he'd seen his brother Alex in June, the sixteen-year-old had lamented the family curse.

"You look good, Mitch," Rat observed as he conducted his horse to a hitching post and secured the reins. "Ain't gone respectable, have you?"

"Only by appearances," Mitch said, laughing. "Got to keep Ma off the scent. Cards haven't let me down yet. We get a lot o' folks through Thayerville now, bound for the new rail spur at Albany or up from Weatherford. There's a stage line stops here."

"Saw the hotel."

"Town's growin'. Fine pickin's on the card tables."

Rat nodded sourly. It didn't seem fair that some should find an easy way to prosperity while others had to claw and scratch money for supper. He couldn't begrudge Mitch, though. Was only fitting one of them should have some good fortune.

"Guess yer cousins still man the counter," Rat mentioned as he followed his old friend toward the mercantile.

"Oh, they've come and gone. She's hired herself the youngest Plank boys now."

"The Planks?" Rat gasped.

"Randy and Vesty. Efrem went and shot the old man last summer. Runs with the Oxenberg brothers."

"Who?"

"Road agents," Mitch explained. "Got 'emselves quite a name hittin' freight wagons and stagecoaches."

"Hereabouts?"

"No, nothin' much happens in Thayerville," Mitch said, sighing. "West o' Albany."

"Strange how things turn out. I never figured Ef for a bandit. Nor killer, either."

"Guess you can't hang a fellow more'n once, and he's wanted for his pa's shootin'."

"Don't see any jury callin' that murder," Rat grumbled. "Ole man's time was overdue."

"Well, enough talk 'bout Plank. Come along. You just won't believe the new place. Got our own house outside o' town, too."

Mitch went on and on as they marched down the street to the new mercantile. Upon arrival, Mitch called for his mother, and Mrs. Morris, true to form, greeted Rat with a bear hug.

"Lord be praised!" she shouted. "I thought you fed to the winds, Rat Hadley. Come meet my new helpers."

"Met 'em before," Rat said, nodding to the Plank boys. They'd grown some, and filled out on Mary Morris's cooking, but Randy's dark, shy eyes were as always. As for Vesty, he dashed over and slapped a husky hand on his one-time defender's back.

"Went and growed up, Vesty," Rat observed as he turned the sixteen-year-old around on his heels. "Miz Morris here workin' you 'nough?"

"Well, she keeps us busy, Randy 'n' me," Vesty answered. "But then you know I never been a stranger to work, and we get to go off to the schoolhouse some."

"Yeah, I worked here myself, you know."

"And at our place, too," Vesty said, dropping his eyes. "Guess you heard Pa's dead. Ma passed on last winter, and he only got worse. Broke Randy's arm and would've kilt him sure if Ef hadn't taken up a shotgun."

"Well, it was a long time comin' by my thinkin'," Rat said, noticing the silent Randy cradling his arm.

"That's about enough serious talk for one day," Mrs. Morris announced. "This is a happy occasion. Come along and see Pa, Rat. He'll never believe you've come home. Wasn't two Sundays past he was remarking how you'd surely got your own ranch by now and a pretty wife to boot."

"Got neither," Rat said, sighing. "Ain't even come by a job."

"Well, that's certain to work itself out," she declared. "Pa knows folks with work to be had. I wouldn't be surprised to discover he knows of something fit."

But Mary Morris's optimism was misplaced. Her husband welcomed Rat warmly enough, but he offered faint hope of finding employment.

"Even a month back there was building going on, but just now it's the lean time of summer, Rat," John Morris reminded the young man. "We hardly do enough business ourselves to merit help in August. In the old days things would pick up once the trail crews came home, but now all the cattle get shipped on the railroad. And the market's sour, Rat. Real sour."

"I know, Mr. Morris. I had ten horses I practically gave away a month back."

"Well, something's sure to come along," Mrs. Morris declared. "Until then you'll stay at the house with us."

"Couldn't do that, ma'am," Rat explained. "I've done my growin'. Cain't take charity."

"Is it charity to take in a boy who's practically kin?" she cried.

"Yes, ma'am," Rat said, thinking of the Plank boys. "I'd say you have plenty o' help, and I'm a long time earnin' my way."

Mrs. Morris started to argue, but her husband motioned her to silence. Rat nodded respectfully, then walked off with Mitch to have a look around Thayerville.

The two old friends spent close to an hour swapping tales of old times and laughing at some foolishness or other perpetrated by the two of them. Then Mitch returned to his gaming table, and Rat stumbled down the street to where his horse was tethered. As he remounted the spry mustang, an unfamiliar voice hailed him.

"Son, you haven't come up from Weatherford, have you?" a short, barrel-chested man in his mid-forties asked.

"Yessir," Rat answered.

"Seen a wagon on your way?"

"Was one," Rat recalled. "Full o' balin' wire and boxes, I think."

"That all? No posts?"

"No, sir," Rat said, scratching his head. "Not as I saw."

"Well, that's a fine thing," the man stormed. "I got fifty miles o' wire to string, and nothing to put it on."

"Sir?" Rat asked. "You mean telegraph wire?"

"Well, it's got no barbs! I've already hired boys to plant the posts, and here I got none, and no pine trees for Lord knows how far."

"Oaks'd pass, or junipers," Rat offered. "I know where a man could cut 'em, and you could haul 'em in with a wagon."

"Do you just? And who exactly would you be, young man?"

"Erastus Hadley," Rat said, "but people call me Rat. I guess I've been across every inch o' this country one time or 'nother. I could cut yer posts if you'd trust me with the work."

"And what would you want for a wage?"

"What the job's worth," Rat answered. "You would've paid somebody for 'em. Pay me instead."

"In need of a job, are you?"

"Bad need," Rat confessed. "Wouldn't be permanent, I know, but maybe later you'd find another use for a man proved handy."

"Might at that, Rat. I'm Sullivan Dawes, out to operate the telegraph here in Thayerville. They call my Sully. You're hired. Now when can you start work?"

"There's light yet today," Rat replied. "Be an hour ridin' to the trees. Start when I get there."

"Well, that's what I like to hear," Dawes declared. "Wait just a minute, though, and I'll hire a wagon. You might as well take the boys along. They can fell trees, I suppose."

"If they cain't, I'll show 'em the trade," Rat promised.

So it was that Rat Hadley went to work for Western Union. Fifty miles meant hundreds of poles, especially along the stretches where the market road crossed open country, and Rat couldn't believe his good fortune. Moreover, building the telegraph line was something a man could take pride in. For once Rat Hadley rode tall.

The work wasn't easy, especially with the sun blazing morning and afternoon, but the air was fresh in the Brazos bottoms, and the company was good. Sully Dawes sent out town boys as he found them, mostly snaggle-toothed teenagers hungry for work and pocket change. Some found felling trees beyond their ability, and others disliked the heat. A freckled redhead named Billy Bedford stuck, though, and he always managed to locate one or two others to help.

60

Finding trees was a challenge, too, especially when they had to be straight. But by prowling here and there, Rat thinned stands of oak and juniper, and the ranchers raised few objections knowing the telegraph would link them with Ft. Worth's swelling stockyards.

Rat and his youthful crew cut thirty posts at a time, then set them at intervals along the Weatherford road. Afterward Sully Dawes inspected the work and satisfied himself the wire and relays were nailed into place. It was while planting posts a dozen miles south of town that Rat got his first peek at a grown-up Becky Cathcart. When Billy identified the visitor, Rat dropped his jaw.

"Cain't be!" he exclaimed.

"I heard you were back," she called from her buggy. "You filled out those shoulders just fine, Rat."

"You done some fillin' yerself, Miss Cathcart. Got the young men buzzin', I'll wager."

"Not so you'd know," she grumbled. "There's a dance at the church Sunday. Care to come?"

"Don't know I got any clothes fit for socializin'."

"They've got suits at the mercantile," she scolded. "You can't go around half naked all your life."

Rat gazed at his sweat-streaked belly and reddened.

"Guess not," Rat confessed as the boys laughed. "I'll get some clothes. Figure we can walk a bit later on?"

"Tomorrow. I'm in Weatherford tonight to visit my aunt. I like looking at the stars, Rat."

"I'm call on you tomorrow," he promised.

The buggy rolled on, and he tossed his hat skyward.

"That's the sheriff's daughter," Billy warned. "You watch you don't get throwed in jail, Rat."

"Sheriff and I been acquainted a long time," Rat assured his young friend. "Saved my life when I was yer size."

"That right?" the redhead asked. "Well, that don't mean he'll let you court his daughter."

Billy turned out to be right. When Rat appeared on the porch of the sheriff's house, a taller Busby Cathcart bid him wait.

"Pa's got words for you, Rat," the boy explained.

"Bus?" Rat asked, confused by the youngster's worried look.

The sheriff then stormed out of the door, clamped a wrist on Rat's arm, and led the way back of the privy.

"I did you a favor once," the lawman pointed out. "Tonight I'll do you another, Rat. Best you move along."

"Sir?" Rat gasped.

"Best you understand how things are, boy. A man comes callin' on a girl, he best have merits."

"Merits?"

"A home," Cathcart explained. "A job with promise. I'll bet the shirt you're wearin' tonight's the first new one you've paid for in a year's time. I got just the one daughter, Rat, and I'll have her happy. You can't offer her that."

"Was just goin' walkin's all," Rat argued.

"Best not make beginnin's when there's no place for it to go, Rat. Mind your place. Elsewise we'll talk again."

The glare in the sheriff's eyes ate into Rat's insides. He turned and stumbled back into town, past the mercantile and the bank and the other marks of civilization. He found his camp and shed his new clothes. You couldn't put a suit on a no-account and make him a man!

Rat kept clear of town afterward. He put his every effort into erecting the telegraph poles, and his only moments of escape were the afternoon swims he shared with Billy and whoever happened to be along that day. On toward the end of September the line was only fifteen miles shy of Weatherford. Rat was wedging a juniper pole into its deep, rocky hole when a voice called his name from the road.

"Still ain't got rid o' them back scars, eh?" Mitch Morris shouted from atop a sleek black gelding.

"Ole Plank put 'em there to remind me who I was," Rat barked without gazing up. "Help me keep my place."

"What's this talk?" Mitch asked. "What place?"

"Oh, he had a visit with the sheriff," Billy explained. " 'Bout Becky."

"Can't take all that to heart, Rat," Mitch argued. "Cathcart won't let me near her, either, and look at me? Have you ever seen such a prosperous fool in all your life?"

"You do look fair, Mitch," Rat admitted with a hint of a grin. Mitch was decked out in a brown suit with vest, and a gold watch chain bobbed in his pocket. Prosperity seemed obvious.

"I'm on my way to Weatherford for a bit o' business," Mitch explained. "Maybe you'd care to join me for some supper at the Station Hotel? I'm buyin'."

"Be late when we finish, Mitch. Maybe another time?"

"I'd come," Billy volunteered. "If yer buyin'."

The other boys added their voices, and Mitch grinned.

"Got to find you civilized company, Rat Hadley. Elsewise you're certain to sprout a tail and stay out here in the rocks forever."

'Least they don't chase me elsewhere, Rat thought as he waved Mitch along down the road. It was hard watching the dust swirls diminish. Harder knowing Mitch was headed somewhere, and Rat Hadley was no better off than one of those juniper poles. He swallowed hard. Would the trail ever turn? Was there nothing better ahead?

Chapter Nine

Rat Hadley devoted himself heart and soul to completing the Thayerville-Weatherford telegraph line. As the last of the poles took its place alongside Station Street, and Sully Dawes spliced two wires to link the two Texas towns, Rat wiped sweat from his forehead. Billy Bedford shouted, and the other youngsters joined in the cheer.

It was later that afternoon, in the telegraph office, when Rat listened to the staccato tapping that Dawes translated into words.

"Test message's come through," the operator told Rat. "Looks like we've built ourselves a telegraph line!"

"Yessir," Rat said, grinning.

"You've done a real fine job for me, son."

"So what's next?" Rat asked. "We goin' out to Albany or maybe over to Jacksboro?"

"Neither," Dawes answered. "I can get a message through to Albany already. I just send through Weatherford, you see. The Ft. Worth line has a spur line up to Jacksboro. All we really needed to communicate with most of the state was to tie into the line at Weatherford."

"Well, must be somethin' for me, Sully," Rat declared. "I done some carpentry. You could use some cabinets in this place, maybe a porch outside."

"That would be for the line manager to decide, Rat. Truth is, I don't have a thing for anybody."

"The boys'll take it hard," Rat said, leaning against the wall.

"Most of them just hired on for pocket money," Dawes responded, "I told Billy I might could use him to run messages."

"I got nothin' lined up myself, Sully."

"Worried that might be, Rat. I can pay you a bonus of ten dollars. Elsewise, well, all I can say is check around."

"I been 'round," Rat explained.

"It's the only advice I know to give," Dawes said, drawing the promised bonus money from an adjacent drawer. "And to wish you luck. Feel free to refer any prospective employer to me. I'll have some good words for them."

"I appreciate that," Rat replied. "Thanks, Sully."

The telegrapher grinned as he passed Rat a pair of five-dollar bank notes. Rat nodded, unsuccessfully trying to hide the disappointment flooding his face.

For a week Rat made his way from one Thayerville enterprise to the next, greeting saloon keeper or blacksmith with equal humility.

"I give Sully Dawes a good day's labor for a fair wage," he assured each one. "I'd give the same to you."

There was always a nephew or a town boy hired to sweep floors or exercise horses, though. And other work simply wasn't to be had.

He next rode among the farms and ranches that occupied the hills and range past town. Rat was startled to discover so many abandoned houses and empty barns. When he did find someone at home, he often had to sidestep idle youngsters and stumble to the door, only to hear the same sad refrain.

"I ain't got work for my own self," tall, gaunt Cyrus Keller explained. "Ain't sold a hog in six months, you know."

"Times is hard," Rat had replied, nodding sadly. And as the days passed, his shoulders sagged and his face grew long. He found himself standing on porches, hat in hand, pleading to speak with ranch foremen or cattlemen.

"Was a time when I'd at least been welcome to sit at table," Rat grumbled to Mitch. "Folks see me comin' and treat me like I got some sickness to give 'em."

"Things'll get better," Mitch assured his haggard friend. "Been out to see Mr. Hanks yet? He's got a high opinion o' you, Rat, from the old days. He's the richest man in the county, after all."

"He sent us packin' after Pa died," Rat recounted. "And didn't take me in after the drive to Kansas."

"Even so, he's out there, Rat. Ain't much o' anybody else."

Rat had to admit the truth of his friend's words. And so that next morning he saddled his horse and rode out to the Circle H to speak with Orville Hanks.

Rat was unusually solemn as he passed the old line cabin that had once been home. He paused a moment, remembering the thunder of boyish laughter, the sound advice offered with fatherly patience, his mother's somber announcement that he must go to live with the Planks.

"Don't suppose it was yer doin', Pa," Rat whispered as he knelt beside his father's grave. The young man stared intently at the simple white cross. Hope and promise, it seemed, were buried along with J. C. Hadley.

Rat's humor wasn't improved by the sight of boys splashing away the morning down at the Brazos. That was *his* river, after all. It would always belong to Rat and Mitch and Alex. These brown-shouldered youngsters were intruders!

Rat splashed across the river, then turned his horse north and west. He didn't answer the waves of the swimmers. Nor did he visit the white oak or Tom Boswell's grave. Rat Hadley needed no reminder that poor fortunes got a man buried.

The sight of a stranger prowling the range on a half-wild mustang wasn't generally welcomed by most outfits, and Rat drew company as he approached the ranch house. First a shaggy-haired young cowboy riding the fence line latched onto Rat's trail. For close to a mile the boy shadowed Rat. Then, as the horse corrals came into view, two older hands confronted Rat. Aside from a tobacco-chewing stranger, a more familiar face challenged the Circle H's visitor.

"Hold up there," Payne Oakley called. "Got business here?"

"Thought to have a word with Mr. Hanks," Rat explained.

"And what makes you think he'd have any interest in seein' you?" Oakley asked.

"Call it old time's sake," Rat answered. "I see you got yer hand healed up, Payne. Bet you never thought I'd get this big, eh?"

"You know him?" the young cowboy asked.

Oakley studied the strange face in front of him. Rat doffed his hat and grinned.

"Can't be," Oakley cried. "Not Rat Hadley!"

"Well, I never knowed anybody else to lay claim to such a name," Rat countered.

"Coley, you run along to the house and fetch Mr. Hanks," Oakley instructed the boy behind them. "Tell him the worst excuse for a wrangler to come out o' Texas's come to see him."

"Sir?" Coley asked.

"Tell him J. C.'s boy is here," Oakley added. "And be quick 'bout it. This particular fellow is apt as not to slip through our fingers. Was forever ridin' off to swim a creek or run some horses when I set him to some other task."

"Sounds familiar," Coley said, grinning at Rat. "I'll be tellin' him, Payne."

Oakley waved his other companion back to work, then escorted Rat to a water tank. They left their horses to have a drink. Then Rat passed ten minutes filling in the ranch foreman on two years of growing and wandering.

"Road's made you hard, Rat," Oakley observed.

"Road's *been* hard, Payne."

"That's a blessin', son. Later on you'll see it so yourself. Easy path leaves a man soft. And this country ain't one to forgive a man's shortcomin's. No, sir. It buries 'em."

"Buried Pa."

"And he was never short o' the mark, Rat. Best kind o' man."

"So I guess bein' hard's not enough. You got to be lucky."

"Well, that helps," Oakley confessed. "But in the final accountin', that ain't enough, neither. Man's got to stand tall when the winds blow."

Rat grinned and shook his head. J. C. Hadley had been a man to talk that way. But hard and tall didn't land a man a job. It was Orville Hanks that would decide that.

Hanks appeared on the broad veranda of his house with two of his sons.

Rat hadn't known any of the Hanks boys very well, what with their being older, and he merely shook their hands politely and agreed to taking after J. C., especially in the face.

"Bandy-legged, too," the elder Hanks observed. "Likely from all them cactus spines you put in your seat mustang huntin'."

"Figured that'd be a long time forgotten," Rat said, laughing. " 'Cept by me, o' course."

"Was the day we lost J. C.," Hanks muttered. "Ain't likely to be forgotten ever. They still call you Rat?"

"With this nose?" Rat asked. "Cursed permanent, you could say."

"Well, it's fittin' not everything's changed. Come walk a way with me, Rat, and tell me what's brought you all the way out here. We don't get many visitors, and most o' them's bill collectors or salesmen."

"I'm neither."

"Nor's it likely after bein' back in these parts weeks and just now comin' here that you come to swap old stories."

"No, sir," Rat admitted. "If you know I've been here, I guess you also know I've been cuttin' telegraph poles and helpin' Sully Dawes string wire."

"Ain't got so old I don't know what's happenin' in this county, Rat."

"Line's finished."

"Know that, too. Know you've been doin' some ridin' hereabouts as well."

"Lookin' for work," Rat explained. "Got some money put by, but not enough to keep me fed through winter. And a man needs somethin' to put his hands to."

"I can't help you, son."

"You know, Mr. Hanks, ain't anybody I'd give leave to call me that. Not with Pa in his grave. But you, and Payne, and maybe Sheriff Cathcart all done a share o' puttin' me on my feet once. You give me a chance to get past hard circumstances and prove myself."

"It's no small pride I take in it, Rat," Hanks confessed. "I've signed on boys aplenty, but few o' them ever measure up. You never give me call to regret takin' you north, nor invitin' you to roundup when you was a grub."

"I thank you for it, too, Mr. Hanks, and I swear you'll have no reason to regret takin' me on again."

"Know that," the cattleman said, frowning. "Rat, you been on the range this last week. What do you see? I sent half my outfit ridin'. Cattle market's gone south, with nary a promise o' returnin' anytime soon."

"I saw boys at the river, and this Coley . . ."

"My grandsons," Hanks explained. "Got my oldest boy Fitz at the line camp now, and near everybody left on the payroll's family. Payroll! We haven't handed out wages in eight months."

"Maybe I could round up some mustangs," Rat offered. "You still need mounts."

"Boy, you ain't listenin'," Hanks complained. "I sell horses nowadays to make my taxes. Even then it's tough to make a price at it. Better you try a town job. Range's dead."

"Have," Rat said, staring at his feet.

"Yeah, not much money to be made anywhere. Funny thing is I thought once the Indians were rounded up and staked out on reservations, cow people'd make their fortunes. Didn't count on all the new land openin' up north and west. Then the railroads come in and take the profit out o' trailin' range beeves. Got to breed 'em now, it 'pears. Takes money, buyin' bulls."

"Mr. Hanks, I've done near everything one time or another. I'd scrub plates or fry eggs."

"Got a cook, Rat. No, your chance'd have to be somewhere else."

"Where?" Rat asked, throwing his arms in the air. "I never in my life begged for help, but I got no other forks in my road. I tried all I know to do, and there's nothin'. Pa used to read me Job, and I always thought it cruel mean for the Lord to send so many torments to one man. Now I don't think ole Job had it so bad after all."

"I read Job some myself," Hanks said, softening his hard-jaw stance. "Lord did relent some where ole Job was concerned. Maybe he's got a heart for wayfarers, too, Rat, 'cause I just thought o' somebody you might try."

"Who?"

"Friend o' mine," Hanks said, pulling a scrap of paper from his shirt pocket and scrawling a note. "Ned Wyler. Operates the Western Stage Company out o' Ft. Worth. Used to run a route to El Paso, but with the Texas and Pacific runnin', they mostly move people up to Jacksboro, then across to Thayerville and along to Albany. He might could use horses, and he might hire you to fetch him some. I done my best by you," he added, passing Rat the note. "You tell him I said you was iron-rumped like yer pa. He finds out you be Corporal J. C. Hadley's kid, he'll do what he can."

"Was this Wyler fellow in yer company, sir?" Rat asked.

"No, he was a Yank colonel," Hanks explained. "Near got his hide peppered when we hit his camp. Yer pa grabbed him by the seat o' the pants and drug him atop a horse. Captured him, ole J. C. did."

"I don't see how that would put me in much favor," Rat argued.

"Wasn't just that," Hanks explained. "We had a stiff-necked major come down and say we got to shoot Colonel Wyler in answer for the Yanks shootin' one o' our officers. Well, yer pa went and liberated Wyler 'fore the major could do it. Next day word come the war was over. General Forrest give up his sword, and we turned for home. Wyler saw we got to the railroad personal. There's a debt owed there."

Rat nodded. *But not to me,* he thought.

Nevertheless he rode south from the Circle H, recrossed the Brazos, and headed east toward Ft. Worth. Three days later he stepped into the office of the Western Stage Company and asked for Ned Wyler.

"I'm Wyler," a burly, bull-necked giant called from behind a cluttered desk. "Who's here to bother me now?"

"Erastus Hadley," Rat announced. "I got a note for you from Orville Hanks."

"Yes?"

"I come lookin' for a job, Colonel Wyler."

"Not many Texans ever call me that," the former officer declared as he accepted the note. "Hanks vouches for you, I see."

Rat studied Wyler's eyes. The note was already crumpled and tossed aside. Devoid of hope, Rat played his final card.

"I'm to tell you Corporal J. C. Hadley was my pa," Rat said.

"Oh," Wyler responded. "Your father did me a great service once. Is this a collection call?"

"Pa's been dead five years," Rat answered angrily. "He never saw need to call on you himself, nor'd he mention what he did to me. Wasn't that way, Pa. If he saved yer neck, it was 'cause he figured there was right to it. So I got no hold on you, Colonel. I'm nineteen years old. I been scratchin' my hold onto life since I can remember. Mr. Hanks said you might could use a man to get you remounts. I got the devil's own way with horses, and I sit a horse better'n most."

"Knowing your father's modesty, that probably means you can outride the devil, too. I don't need stock handlers, Hadley."

"I dug holes for telegraph poles up in Thayerville, and cut the poles, too. I could build you corrals or . . ."

"They're built. I don't need diggers or woodcutters. It does happen I need a stagecoach guard for the westbound run out of Thayerville and the eastbound back from Albany. Ever fire a gun?"

"Since I could hold one," Rat replied.

"Ever hit anything?"

"Only what I aim at," Rat said with blazing eyes.

"Such as?"

"Shot a rattler at a hundred yards when I was seven. A bull buffalo at ten. Been hittin' things ever since."

"Ever shoot a man?"

"Once," Rat said, frowning.

"Tell me about it," Wyler urged, stepping closer and listening with new interest.

"Was on the trail drive north," Rat explained. "First time I ever fired a handgun 'cept at targets. Raiders come at us, and I was atop a hill with my buddy Mitch Morris."

"And?"

"Riders charged. I aimed at a boy no older'n I was and kilt him with my first shot. Didn't see it then, not with the smoke and all. Later, though, I saw him dead with my bullet 'tween his eyes."

"Shoot at anybody since then?"

"Never had a need, Colonel."

"Nor the desire?"

"You been a soldier, sir. You got any such desires?"

"No, I've seen enough dead men."

"So've I," Rat growled.

"If you were to sign on with me, Hadley, you'd likely have call to shoot again. We've had trouble."

"You'd pay me to shoot men. That it?"

"To protect the coach. If you never hit a man, I wouldn't care. Only you'd have to keep them clear of our coaches and protect the passengers. If it came down to that, could you do it?"

"If he was after me and mine, yessir, I think so."

"Not sure?"

"Can anybody be?"

"Well, that's honest enough. We'll give you a try. Pay's twenty dollars a week. You see Nate Parrott in Thayerville. That's your home, I take it."

"Sort of."

"Give him this letter," Wyler said, scrawling a note. "Tuesday next you ride the westbound to Albany. Next day you return on the eastbound. Got that? Runs twice a week that way."

"Fair enough."

"Off days you help at the freight office."

"Yessir."

"If you like, Nate can put you up in the stable loft. Save you a few dollars if you don't mind the company of horses."

"I'm pretty used to 'em," Rat confessed. "People never've much taken to me."

"A bath and a shave'll help that. Here's your first week's pay. See if you can't come by some shirts and a pair of trousers that fit. Keep the gambling and drinking out of your way, too. I expect the straight and narrow, Hadley."

"Yessir."

"One more thing. Good luck to you."

"Luck and me's strangers, Colonel. But I'll make out fine just the same. I won't disappoint you."

Wyler nodded, and Rat imagined he would have to fall mighty short of the mark to lose the colonel's confidence. Sometimes you could tell things in a man's eyes. And the burly Wyler was almost smiling.

Chapter Ten

The Western Stage Company operated out of a small plank building between the bank and the hotel. There were three tiers of shelves for storing freight in back, with a narrow counter up front for selling tickets and conducting the freight business. Out back a small stable housed remounts and such employees as had no other place to bed.

When Rat stepped inside, he was greeted warmly by a slight-shouldered clerk in his late twenties.

"I'm Nate Parrott," he said. "Can I sell you a ticket to Albany?"

"No, I brought you a note from Colonel Wyler," Rat explained. The clerk accepted the crumpled paper and read it quickly. A smile appeared on his face.

"Glad to have you," Parrott announced. "We been makin' do with stray cowboys or nobody at all. I've been scared to trust any money to the coach, what with the trouble others have had along the river."

"You the new guard then?" a heavy-set stranger called from the shelves.

"For a time anyhow," Rat answered.

"Yer young," the big man observed. "Used to work for the Morrises, I'm guessin'."

"Yessir," Rat said, searching his memory for the name that matched the face.

"You wouldn't remember. I only came into the store 'round plantin' time back then. Was farmin'."

"Meet Hoyt Palmer," Parrott told Rat. "Hoyt's your driver. Hoyt, this is Erastus Hadley."

"Erastus," Palmer said, stepping closer and offering his meaty hand. "Most everybody calls me Pop. I got four youngsters at home, you see, and you cain't be so much older'n the eldest."

"They call me Rat," Rat replied. "Not much recommendation, I know, but it's easier."

"You two'll get better acquainted Tuesday," Parrott declared. "Rat, you take the westbound to Albany, then bring the eastbound back here. Twice a week."

"The colonel told me."

"Meanwhile we can use your help in the storeroom. Be a full load we haul west this week. Everything from candles to a weddin' dress."

"More next time," Palmer added. "Nobody's trusted us with money lately, not ridin' short on guard. Guess that'll change."

Rat nodded. He hoped not to disappoint them.

As things turned out, Rat had little difficulty settling into his new job as stagecoach guard. He sat atop the coach alongside Hoyt Palmer, cradling a long Winchester rifle and keeping his eyes on the countryside ahead, behind, and to each side. The first trip proved uneventful, and Rat yawned with weariness as the coach rumbled along the rough trail. Soon dust stirred by the horses clung to every inch of him, ate at his collar, near choked him.

"Think this is somethin'?" Palmer asked. "Ought to travel this country in July. Heat and dust close to drive a man mad!"

Rat could believe it. The boredom worked its own mischief. And the only distraction came from Hoyt Palmer's wild yarns or his endless tales of one child or another.

"The boys's somethin', Rat," he'd begin. "Tyler's closin' fast on fourteen now, and he has nigh every gal in the county chasin' him. The younger ones, Hollis and Wade, they got the quickness I never come by. Take after my Varina, I guess. The jewel's Velma, though. Twelve she is, and already bloomin' like a rose. Be a stampede o' boys comin' to my door soon, I tell you."

"A family's a real comfort," Rat observed.

"Oh, it can vex you, too. Like last week when Hollie went and put a horned toad down his sister's back. And I caught the three boys swipin' pie crusts off ole widow Morgan a month back. Switched 'em raw that time. But you know boys. They got the mischief in their blood, and it's bound and certain to come out here and there."

Rat didn't answer. He recalled his own escapades at the river with Mitch, but all that seemed a lifetime away now. And as his eyes swept the distant trees or searched the boulder-littered hills, he found scant reason to grin.

For weeks Rat accompanied Hoyt Palmer on the trail from Thayerville to Albany. Each trip was less eventful than the one before. The biggest excitement came when Palmer surprised the Circle H cowboys in their midafternoon swim. Rat only fired his rifle once, and that was at a rampaging longhorn bull that blocked the trail. The Winchester persuaded the animal to yield his ground.

Autumn had painted the oaks scarlet, and there was a late October bite to the wind the day Rat detected riders shadowing the stage on its westward leg toward Albany. He counted three in plain view, and he supposed others might be elsewhere. One moved to cut the coach off on its approach toward a narrow gap between the rocky hills, and Rat readied his rifle for the confrontation.

"No point to us makin' a fight o' it," Palmer argued. "We only got some dry goods aboard. Only passenger's that gambler Horton and the Reilly twins."

"Drive, Pop!" Rat shouted as he fired a warning shot at the horsemen.

"Lord, help us!" Palmer cried as he lashed the horses into a gallop.

It didn't take a genius to recognize a tight spot. As the stage raced ahead, Rat detected two men riding hard in its wake. The three he'd seen before assembled up ahead and pulled flour sacks down over their heads to mask their faces. Fierce eyes seemed to bore through narrow slits in the masks, and a bullet nicked the brake. Another tore a slice from the right hand door.

"Get down low!" Rat yelled as one of the Reilly youngsters poked a shaggy head out of the open window. The gambler fired off his pistol. Rat crawled up among the freight boxes on top of the coach and steadied his aim. He fired twice, and the pursuing horsemen faltered. The lead rider's horse collapsed with a bullet through its neck, and the second man nursed a shattered arm.

"You got 'em, boy!" the gambler cheered, and the Reilly boys added their own howls.

Up ahead the danger remained, for several bullets now slammed into the coach. Rat's well-laid fire scattered the attackers, though, and the coach roared past the cursing outlaws.

"We made it!" Palmer yelled as he glanced back at the frustrated bandits.

"This time," Rat observed. For after all, the raiders had split their forces, and they tipped their hand early. But then they probably hadn't expected a guard—at least not Rat Hadley!

When the westbound pulled into Albany, the Reilly twins wasted no time in spreading an exaggerated tale of the raid.

"Was ten o' them at least!" one twin shouted. "Mr. Hadley kilt three o' them and chased th'others clear. He's a regular hero, I tell you."

The gambler was less sure of the death toll, but he was equally generous with his praise.

"Did a fine job, young man," the gambler said when he passed Rat a twenty-dollar gold piece. "You didn't know I had a season's winnin's with me, I'll bet. Two thousand dollars!"

"So that's what set 'em on our trail," Palmer noted. "Wondered 'bout that."

"Likely the bunch I took at the card tables," the gambler supposed. "Didn't press things like real road agents."

"They was real enough," Palmer said, pointing to the bullet holes peppering the coach. "And if they knew you, it's certain they'd kilt the all o' us."

"Lord bless you, Mr. Hadley," Opal Reilly called.

"You enjoy yer blessin'," Palmer said. "For a real thank you, let's hop on over to the White Horn Saloon. You got a drink comin'."

"I don't take much hard liquor," Rat argued as he helped a pair of freight handlers unload the Albany-bound crates.

"I'd say you earned a bit this time," Palmer replied. "And 'bout the time it sinks into yer head what you done, I'm sure o' it."

"Go on," a growing crowd urged. "Here's to Deadeye Hadley!"

"Calls himself Rat," someone objected. "Rat Hadley."

"Well, let's share a drink with the rat then," a voice called. "Eh?"

And so Rat was swept across the street by a gang of thirty townsfolk, and he ended up sipping three fiery thimbles of whiskey before he slumped dizzily in a chair.

"Fine shot, but he sure ain't used to spirits," Palmer noted. "Give me some room, boys. Best I carry him along to the stable to sleep it off."

For a hero to suffer as much as Rat Hadley did that eve and the following morn seemed patently unfair. No sooner had Pop Palmer carried him to the Western Company's stable than Rat was heaving up his insides. To make matters worse, his head felt as if someone had taken a twenty-pound sledge to it.

"Guess you ain't had no chance to accustom yerself to Brazos tater wine," Palmer said, laughing as Rat rolled his eyes. "Best stick to beer till yer gullet grows taller."

"If it has a chance," Rat grumbled.

"It will," the big driver assured him. "Anyhow, get some rest, Rat. We take the eastbound home tomorrow."

Rat only sighed and collapsed in the hay, hoping sleep might offer escape from the whiskey's aftermath. In truth, it did. The next dawn found Rat's head ringing, and his eyes red as tomatoes.

"Get 'em cleared up fast," Palmer urged. "We're off in half an hour."

Rat passed the return journey in a cloud. Each jolt of the coach set his head to pounding, and his stomach refused to tolerate food. Fortunately the raiders were also recovering, and the trip passed peacefully.

The coach's arrival in Thayerville was another matter. No sooner had the wheels rolled to a halt than people rushed out of shops and saloons to cheer their homegrown hero.

"All I done was throw a few shots at 'em," Rat complained.

"Saved two children from certain death, as I heard it," Varina Palmer proclaimed. "And brought my man back to the bosom of his family."

Rat had to grin at the sight of a petite Varina Palmer hugging her giant of a husband. A smallish, plain-faced girl joined them, as did three bony-legged boys. It was hard to believe the children were the same ones Pop had described in his numerous tales. But young Tyler wrapped an eager arm around Rat and thanked him for saving his father, and Varina provided a generous invitation to supper that night.

"From now on there'll be no stable sleepin', either," the woman insisted. "Ty's made you up a rope bed in the boys' room, and you'll pass your nights in Thayerville with us."

Rat started to argue, but the Palmers wouldn't have it. And once he tasted Varina's pork chops, he had no urge to object. He clearly saw how Hoyt Palmer had increased his girth, and if the children were plain and a bit ragged, they were nevertheless full of pepper and noise. They howled with delight at every tale Rat spun of his years on the range. In contrast to the silence of the stable, Pop Palmer's crowded farmhouse was a home.

Nate Parrott provided a few rewards of his own.

"Colonel Wyler sent you his congratulations, Rat," the stationmaster explained the next day. "You got yourself five dollars a week more money, and the colonel says to pick out the best pair o' handguns you can spot. They're on him."

"I never handled nothin' fancy," Rat explained. "Just this ole Colt give to me on the cattle drive north."

"I'll help you choose 'em," Parrott pledged. "I already spoke to Mary Morris at the mercantile 'bout some new clothes, too. Colonel wired we got to outfit you proper."

"I don't understand," Rat complained. "All I did was what you hired me for. I just shot a horse and drove off some fellows who likely weren't but broke cowboys tryin' to get their poker money back."

"Not how others see it, Rat. You already brung us business. From here on out there'll be lots o' money travelin' to Albany and back, I wager."

"Won't make my job any easier, will it?"

"Sure won't. Honey draws flies, you know. Now run along to the mercantile. I got work for you after."

Rat nodded, then started out the door. As he walked, he couldn't help shaking his head to clear the cobwebs. Any minute he expected to wake up in the stable having dreamed the whole business.

Vesty Plank was tending the counter when Rat appeared.

"Always knew you hadn't any sense," the boy declared. "Takin' on Pa the way you did back when. Took my lickin' that time, Rat. And now . . ."

"I'm supposed to pick out some clothes," Rat explained.

"Miz Morris got 'em ready for you, all 'cept the size. Rat, you got to be careful here on out."

"What?"

"Ef rides with some folks out past Albany," Vesty explained. "I hear things sometimes. You watch out, hear?"

"Thanks, Vesty," Rat said, giving the frail young man a shake of the shoulders. "I know those words didn't come easy."

"No, but I owed you," he said, gazing intently into Rat's eyes. "I seen Pa shot, too. Bullets make big holes in people, Rat. And it don't matter if a man acts brave or not."

Rat nodded his agreement as Mary Morris arrived. With a shout, she rushed over and hugged Rat tightly.

"Lord be praised!" she shouted. "My boy's been delivered from peril. You should quit that stage company, Rat Hadley. It's not God's work, shooting men."

"Maybe not, ma'am, but it's work just the same," he answered. "I had no rush o' other offers. Seems to me, ma'am, like the Lord sends a man on his way. I see the path, and I take my steps along it. All I know to do."

"Nothing good ever came of violence," she argued.

"Seems to me people look me in the eye now. That's a middlin' good, don't you think? I ain't much, Miz Morris, but nobody ought to step on me like they used to. They don't try it now. And they won't long as I keep ridin' the stage."

"And when someone shoots you dead?"

He tried to manage a smile. He wanted to tell her how the pain would end. Instead he kept mum and let her show him the clothes she'd picked out.

Chapter Eleven

Rat Hadley was outfitted in new woolen trousers, a cotton shirt, and a heavy sheepskin coat when he climbed up beside Pop Palmer for the westbound journey to Albany that next day. The two elderly women in the coach paid him no mind, and Pop merely chewed the remainder of one of Varina's biscuits. Glory and fame were apparently short-lived.

The westbound trip proved as dull and uneventful as any Rat could recall. In spite of a sharp wind that left him half-numb, he maintained a close watch on the surrounding countryside. Once or twice he thought he detected shadows in the rocks, but they never sprouted faces or rifles. It proved a peaceful crossing.

The return leg of the trip seemed different from the first. To begin with, the coach was crowded with passengers. Roy and Tobin Heathcock, a pair of Ft. Worth merchants, were finishing a hide-buying trip with a swing through Brazos towns. Mrs. Ethel Gardiner and her two children were off to see family in Thayerville, and one of the Albany freight handlers, young Ed Robson, had talked Colonel Wyler into providing a free trip home to see an ailing mother.

"Got a full load this trip," Palmer grumbled as he heaved a money chest up to Rat. A second chest followed. Ned Wyler had designed his coaches with a small compartment below the driver's bench where chests could be concealed, and Rat saw the chests placed there side by side. It made sense to hide valuables, but Rat judged half the state knew about the hidden space now.

"Figure to run into trouble?" Rat whispered as Palmer took his place atop the coach.

"Never think elsewise, Rat," the driver answered. "Don't like to be disappointed. If we have a clear run, well, that's just fine. You plan on trouble, you don't go losin' yer head when she comes 'long."

Rat deemed it a truth. And as they headed eastward, he checked his rifle and prepared for the worst.

Rat first saw the outlaws ten miles from Albany. There were just two of them, but their flour-sack masks testified to their intent. Rat motioned toward them with his rifle, and Palmer frowned.

"We could turn round," Rat suggested.

"If we want to close this line," Palmer muttered. "We see 'em good. Ones to worry over's them you don't see."

Rat nodded his agreement. That was already troubling him.

For a time the stage seemed to lose its shadowing riders. The pair kept to the hills. Whenever they got within range of the Winchester, Rat fired, and they skedaddled back to safety.

"What you doin', boy?" Roy Heathcock barked from the window just below. "Shootin' squirrels?"

"No, snakes," Rat answered. "Curious kind."

"There's robbers chasin' us!" little Tully Gardiner cried. "I seen 'em. You get one o' them, mister?"

"Just seein' they stay respectable back," Rat answered.

So they remained for the better part of the crossing. It wasn't until they started down a hillside just south of the Brazos that real trouble came. The narrow trail was blocked by a rockslide.

"Any way 'round?" Rat asked.

"Nope," Palmer replied. "Got to clear the trail."

Palmer pulled the coach to a halt, and Rat clambered down.

"Ed, come lend yer back," Rat urged as he tossed a small rock aside. The Heathcocks joined in the effort to remove the obstructing rocks. Rat did his best to scan the hills on either side of the trail for faces, but there were moments when his back was needed more than his shooting eye. It took every man there to pry a pair of boulders from the road. Even as the second of the big rocks rolled away, shots rang out.

"Tobe!" Roy Heathcock screamed as he fell back clutching his belly.

"Roy!" Tobin answered as he hurried to help his stricken brother. Mrs. Gardiner ushered her children to cover, and Rat pulled young Robson out of the way. Pop Palmer was already scurrying under the coach.

"Got real trouble this time," Palmer declared as Rat eyed his rifle resting beside the door of the coach.

"Can you reach the Winchester?" Rat asked.

"I can," Tully Gardiner answered, jumping out and grabbing the rifle as three shots erupted from the high ground above. The boy dragged the rifle to Rat and gazed up proudly at the guard.

"Get down, fool boy," Rat cried, forcing the youngster behind a rocky refuge. "They're shootin' real bullets, you know."

"Yeah, but I'm quick," Tully boasted. "I can shoot, too."

"Not this day," Rat said, covering the foolhardy mop of amber hair with a weary hand. "Ed, you all right?"

"Scared out o' my hide, but no holes in me."

"How're the Heathcocks?"

"One of 'em's bad," Ed answered. "Other one's just mad."

Rat stared at the hills on either side of the trail. It was well-laid, this ambush. And he was caught in it like a rabbit snared in a dead fall.

"Give it up!" a voice boomed from above them. "You got no chance!"

Rat turned to Pop Palmer, but the driver shrugged his shoulders and gazed helplessly.

"I plan to get Mr. Heathcock inside the coach," Rat explained. "Pop, you look after Tully here. If we get the others inside, you climb up and get us movin'. Long as we're down here, we got no chance."

Rat made his way over to the Heathcocks. Roy was breathing heavily, and his clothes were soaked with blood. He was clearly dying, but his brother would not leave him behind.

"This is how we'll do it," Rat began. "Ed, take this pistol. You help the Heathcocks, then watch the north hillside. I'll cover you and keep the south ridge clear."

"Boy, you're crazy," Tobin Heathcock objected. "They've got us. Do as they say and we got a chance."

"Ain't many o' them," Rat argued. "Two chased us in, and I count maybe one or two other rifles. Don't have enough fire or they'd taken us by now."

"Might have help comin'," the merchant pointed out.

"Well, we may have some ourselves," Rat muttered.

Nobody seemed very eager to follow a stumpy nineteen-year-old's orders, but there wasn't any other plan. Rat nodded to his companions, then darted forward, He raised the Winchester to his shoulder and opened up on the far slope. Ed Robson helped Tobin Heathcock drag his injured brother along to the coach. Meanwhile rifle fire descended from both sides upon the coach.

It was momentary madness. Bullets splintered rock and sliced into the stagecoach. The horses reared and stomped in an effort to free themselves from the confines of their harness. One figure made a move down the south hill, but Rat sent him scrambling back to safety. Then two rifle bullets chased Rat from cover, and a third tore through his left arm.

"Rat?" Palmer called.

"I'm all right," Rat screamed as he dove behind another boulder and dragged his rifle along. He felt the blood running up his arm and soaking his sheepskin coat, but there was no time for making repairs.

"Give it up down there!" the outlaw leader urged. "You got no chance."

"Come down and see what chance we got!" Rat barked.

"Don't need to, friend," the voice on the hillside answered. "We can wait you out, come by dark."

"Can you?" Rat responded. "When this coach doesn't reach town, Sheriff Cathcart's sure to send a posse."

"Won't do you no good. Y'all be dead then."

"We got Miz Gardiner to think of," Palmer called. "Rat?"

"No!" Rat yelled as he painfully fired his rifle. He then motioned Palmer to climb up and started toward the coach himself.

The outlaws hesitated just a moment. It was what Rat had hoped for. Tully Gardiner scrambled inside, and Palmer lumbered up and retook the reins. Even as Rat tossed his rifle up and followed, the raiders suddenly descended.

"Get 'em!" the leader yelled.

Rat lifted the Winchester with his right hand and managed to steady the barrel. A masked figure filled the sights, and Rat fired. A bullet knocked the thief's feet from beneath him. A pistol shot from the coach drove off a second outlaw.

"Rat, behind you!" Palmer shouted as he whipped the horses into motion.

Rat had but a second to act. He whirled and saw a solitary masked bandit clamber up the side of the coach. The outlaw pointed the cold barrel of his pistol toward Rat's face, but Rat managed to knock the gun aside using the Winchester's barrel. Then, as the surprised raider frantically threw himself atop the coach, Rat discarded his rifle and drew the remaining pistol from his twinned holsters.

"Shoot!" Palmer shouted, and Rat rammed back the hammer with his thumb and fired a single round through the attacker's forehead. The masked figure collapsed in a heap amid the neatly arranged trunks and boxes.

"You got him!" Palmer cried. "Rat, you got him!"

"Sure, I did," Rat said, trembling as he glanced back and watched the remaining outlaws falling far behind. "Now get this coach to town. Hurry!"

Rat occupied himself that next hour and a half stemming the blood flowing out of his arm. Already he was growing light-headed, and he could barely keep his eyes open. Danger remained, of course, for the raiders had horses. In the end, though, the Western Company's eastbound rolled into Thayerville without further incident.

The coach had hardly stopped when Tobin Heathcock jumped out and called for a doctor. Onlookers stared at the bullet holes in the side of the coach, and soon a crowd gathered. Nate Parrott sent a boy off to locate Dr. Tom Jennings, and a party of men managed to carry Roy Heathcock inside the stage office.

"Never mind about the doc," someone announced. "That fellow needs buryin'."

"Not yet!" Tobin objected.

But when the doctor arrived, he pronounced Roy Heathcock dead.

"Can't you boys check a pulse?" Doc Jennings complained.

"Trip's not wasted, Doc," Tully Gardiner announced, helping his mother out of the coach. "Ma caught some splinters, and Josie there's got herself nicked, too."

"Nothin' we can't tend to," the doctor assured the boy.

"Rat's got himself shot, too," Pop Palmer said, pointing to the pale guard slumped across the driver's bench.

"Who's that up there with the cases?" the doctor asked.

"One o' the ones that hit us," Palmer explained. "Was young Rat did it!"

Sheriff Cathcart parted the crowd and climbed up atop the coach. He tore away the mask and then handed down the corpse.

"Well, I'll be hanged!" Parrott exclaimed. "It's Curly Bob Clark."

"It is!" Ed Robson agreed. "I seen his posters."

"There's five-hundred dollars reward out on him," Cathcart added. "Made yourself a rich man this day, Rat. Rat?"

A dozen hands reached up and drew Rat Hadley down from the coach. There were no mocking grins or cruel taunts now, though. An odd sort of respect flooded the crowd of faces.

"You folks'll put him in an early grave!" Doc Jennings complained as he examined Rat's shattered arm. "Get him along to my place, why don't you? He's near bled to death!"

"Pick him up, boys. Get him over to Doc's," the sheriff barked. "Hurry."

The entire town seemed out on Main Street now, and the best part of the people migrated to Doc Jennings's surgery. To Rat it was all a blur, though. He felt a ringing in his ears, and a terrible numbness began to take possession of him.

No! he wanted to shout. Death wouldn't, couldn't be so cruel as to steal him away now, in his one moment of triumph!

Cold fingers seemed to grip his lungs, though, and breathing was terribly hard. He could feel his heart pounding, but his feet and legs were ice. Then a great haze enveloped him, and he drifted away.

Chapter Twelve

Rat awoke to a world of fuzzy shapes. He lay in a hard slat bed in the side room of an unfamiliar house. As the dizziness began to pass, he detected a wash basin atop a small wooden stand, a window framed by simple gingham check curtains, and a solitary chest standing on the far wall beside an open door. Sitting in a chair beside him was a boy of around twelve years, whose curly yellow hair and bright blue eyes seemed out of place in the drab chamber.

"You awake, Rat?" the youngster asked.

"Parts o' me," Rat confessed, raising his head slightly. His left side felt as if nailed to the bed, and his legs remained asleep.

"Doc said you'd come 'round this mornin'. Me, I figured it'd be later on."

"Where . . ."

"At our place." Seeing Rat's confusion, the boy laughed to himself and explained further. "Guess it's changed some since you come here last time. Five years."

"Where . . ." Rat began again.

"Don't you recognize me?" the youngster asked with slightly hurt eyes. "I'm Busby Cathcart."

"Yeah?" Rat whispered. "Well, ain't seen you much o' late. Changed some, too."

"Gotten ornery, Pa says. He's been by to see you, but you was sleepin'."

"How long?"

"Been two days since Doc plucked that bullet out o' your arm. You bled all over the place, he said. Pa thought you dead sure, but not Becky. She ordered you brought over here, and she took to tendin' you herself. 'Cept at night and early morn. I saw to you then, this bein' my room and all."

"Thanks," Rat managed to mutter as he blinked his eyes. The feeling was returning bit by bit. He saw he was lying between crisp linen sheets. His head rested on a feather pillow. His left arm was swathed in bandages. Otherwise he was naked.

"You up to sippin' some broth?" Busby asked. "Ma can heat you up some. Or you can wait for Becky to come along."

"Where'd my clothes get to?" Rat interrupted.

"Doc fair butchered your shirt, Rat. The rest was pretty much bloody. Ma give 'em a scrub, but it wasn't much use."

"I've got some things over at Pop Palmer's house. Maybe you could . . ."

"That's a fine idea," Rebecca Cathcart announced as she entered the room. "Buzz, why don't you walk over there and collect Rat's clothes. He's sure to be here a week."

"Meanwhile Pa's got a nightshirt he can spare," Busby declared. "Makes a man unsettled to have women hoverin' 'round 'em, 'specially when he's got only a sheet for cover. And I wouldn't let her give you no more baths, neither, Rat!"

"What?" Rat cried. His mind seemed to clear of cobwebs, and he drew the sheet up against his chin with the fingers of his good right hand. Busby only laughed and darted off.

"Don't look so shocked," Becky said as she took her brother's place beside the bed. "I've done my share o' bathin' people, boys included. Wish I had a silver dollar for every time I washed Buzz. I've got cousins, too, remember."

"So've I, but I never gave 'em any bath," Rat grumbled. "They weren't full-grown, either."

"Well, I admit this was my first turn at a full-sized one," Becky said, grinning shyly. "Ma would've done it, but she was off somewhere, and you were just about covered up with mud and blood. Doc said you needed scrubbin' then and there. I wager there'll be talk come o' it, though."

"Likely so," Rat said, swallowing his embarrassment and thinking of the string bean of a girl washing away the aftermath of battle. "I fear yer reputation's soiled. Havin' dealin's with no-account Hadleys ain't a thing folks forget easy."

"Oh, that's a long time forgotten, Rat."

"Is it? Yer own pa spoke to me 'bout stayin' clear o' you just lately."

"Did he?" she asked, surprised. "Well, he's changed that tune, Rat. Wouldn't hear o' the Morrises takin' you in. You set too much stock in gossip anyhow. And the truth o' it is most o' the town folk'd have us headed to an altar."

"That'd surely be a worse fate for you'n havin' 'em gossipin', Becky. Bein' chained to Rat Hadley! Best you leave my nursin' to Busby."

"He'd make short work o' you. And besides, I don't know I'd agree marryin' a hero'd be such a poor bargain."

"Hero?"

"Sure," she said, smiling. "The man who shot Curly Bob Clark and saved the Western Stage. You've gone and gotten famous, Rat. And rich to boot. Curly Bob was posted, you know."

Rat shook his head in dismay. He only recalled bits and pieces of the fight, and nothing at all of its aftermath. Becky laughed and retold the whole story, borrowing liberally from the boastful stories of Ed Robson and Tully Gardiner. Envisioning himself as a rifle-toting gunman was too far a stretch for Rat, though, and he welcomed Busby Cathcart's return for putting a close to the wild tale.

As he mended those next days, Rat started to realize the better part of Thayerville believed every exaggerated word of that story. The Gardiners paid him a visit on the return leg of their journey, bringing along copies of a Ft. Worth newspaper detailing his gallant exploits. Ed Robson provided a small packet of telegrams from folks expressing their high regards for him. One or two offered jobs. Colonel Ned Wyler paid a bonus and promised a full wage while Rat was recovering his health.

"Don't hurry yerself none," Pop Palmer explained. "Colonel told me so himself. Likely he'll come along and tell you the same thing one o' these days. Business's been pickin' up, what with Curly Bob planted."

Doc Jennings soon cut away the dressing and drained Rat's wound. Afterward Busby Cathcart brought friends by to stare at the scar or shake hands with Thayerville's new hero. Rat did so with as straight a face as he could manage and afterward chuckled to himself.

Mitch Morris appeared every evening, bringing bits of news or something his mother sent over from the mercantile.

"Things've sure changed, Rat," Mitch observed. "Ma's got nothing but fine words for you. Me, I walk the devil's road. You get yerself well, hear? I got nobody to swap tales with or chase through the river."

But of all his visitors, Rat most appreciated the quiet hours he spent with Becky Cathcart. When others were around, the seventeen-year-old seemed full of jests and energy. But when they were alone, Rat discovered she possessed a serious nature. She shared books and spoke of the trials that perhaps lay ahead. And every once in a while they dared to reveal dreams.

"I won't be ridin' guard on a stagecoach forever," Rat vowed. "I figure to have a little place o' my own, maybe run horses and some cows. Nothin' like the Circle H, mind, but a good solid future for me and mine."

"Me, I'd like to teach school somewhere," Becky confided. "I'd want a good husband to love and care for, and children to raise. Maybe we'd have a little place off from town, like this house. Little ones need some room to run, don't you think? In town they grow up too fast, I'm thinkin'."

"They grow up too fast lots o' places," Rat muttered, recalling his days at the Plank farm. "Overnight sometimes."

She recognized the pain in his eyes and provided a comforting hand. Her quiet nod acknowledged understanding, and it endeared him to her even more.

Rat was a week on his back at the Cathcart place. Later, when he walked about, his left arm hanging limply in a cloth sling, he contributed what he could to his new family. One day he sliced tomatoes. Another time he mixed dough and made a batch of one-handed biscuits.

"I'm astounded," Cora Cathcart cried when she tasted one of the flaky discs. "They're just fine, Rat."

"You make a fair cook," the sheriff added.

"Well, you pick up a thing or two on yer own," Rat told them.

"We've no need of learnin' just what," Becky declared.

Busby grinned. The sheriff and his wife exchanged knowing looks. An hour later Lemuel Cathcart led Rat out to the porch.

"I know what's on yer mind, Sheriff," Rat said, avoiding the lawman's steel-eyed gaze. "I'm on my feet again, and the wound's clean-scabbed. Time I was packin' up and movin' on."

"Son?" Cathcart asked, stepping closer. "What makes you think that?"

"I ain't altogether stupid," Rat muttered. "Since Pa died, folks've been takin' me aside, urgin' me to move on. You get to where you see it comin'."

"You're wrong this time, Rat."

"Am I? Didn't you tell me yer feelin' where Becky's concerned? Well, I didn't plan it out this way, you know. Did I ask you to bring me here, to have her carin' for me? You should've left me at the doc's. I got a fair share o' strong feelin' for her, Sheriff. Ain't no backin' away from it."

"I don't suppose you figure this town's given you much of a chance, eh, Rat?"

"Has it?"

"And me?"

"You saved my life when you took me off the Plank place," Rat said, frowning as the memories flooded his mind. "I was all cold inside then, dead more'n alive. You and the Morrises put me back on my feet. Now you've gone and done it again. I know you'd rather Becky turned her eyes in other directions. And I guess if you say the word, I'll do my best to step aside. Be like cuttin' out my heart, but I'd try. I owe you that."

"Rebecca's closin' in on her eighteenth birthday, son," the sheriff replied. "She's full grown and sure to make her own choices. As are you."

"And so far as the two o' us . . ."

"Look, Rat, so long as you're honest with her, and you do her no wrongs, you'll have nothin' to answer me for. Whether you think so or not, I've always liked you. It's been a steep trail you've had to climb, but you made it to the top as I see it. I expect you'll find others deem it so, too."

"I got some hard memories," Rat confessed.

"I can't see how it'd be otherwise. I've heard half the boys in Thayerville describe the scar on your arm. That's the easy one to see, though, isn't it. It'll fade by and by. The long healin' ones are deep down, and some o' them never do mend. I think Thayerville's offerin' you a fresh start, though, Rat. Maybe some think it should've been given before, but what's done is done. You've got some money comin' for Curly Bob, and the stage line's certain to hold you in high esteem for some time to come. That's the kind o' future I hope lies in store for Busby. It's the man I hope he grows to be."

"I take that for high praise," Rat declared.

"Was meant to be," Cathcart declared. "Rat, you stay on here as long as you like. Buzz likes havin' company in the side room, and it won't be much longer you're operatin' one-armed. Later, once you mend, you may care to move to the hotel. But should you choose to remain, well, nobody'd be displeased."

"Nobody at all," Rat added. The sheriff smiled, and Rat felt warmer inside than anytime he could recall.

The following afternoon the promised reward arrived, together with an extra twenty-dollar bounty Ned Wyler brought in person. The Colonel inspected Rat's arm personally.

"You look fit, Hadley, but a stagecoach does a fair degree of bouncing. Give it another week before you climb up with that Winchester."

"I pass another week useless, I'll go daft," Rat confessed.

"Nothin' to keep you from mindin' the freight office, is there? Don't tote anything heavy, but you can watch out for trouble. I'll pass the word to Nate Parrott."

"I appreciate that, Colonel," Rat answered.

Rat's return to work wasn't the only sign of his healing. That next Sunday, following services at the new Methodist Church, the reverend announced plans for a barn dance.

"Think you're up to it, Rat?" Becky asked as she led the way to her father's waiting buggy.

"I got no talent for the steps," Rat grumbled, recalling his Kansas misfortunes. "But I'm willin' to try."

"I'll show you the steps," she assured him. "And you can't be any worse a dancer than Buzz. I spent half the last dance with him, you know. We've got a shortage o' unmarried men in the town o' Thayerville."

He grinned and promised his best efforts. But when the time came, Rat Hadley proved a failure. He had trouble leading Becky and watching her show him the steps at the same time. Twice they tangled badly, and once they wound up in a heap surrounded by a crowd of laughing neighbors.

"Busby, give you sister a break from this young tanglefoot, will you?" the sheriff finally said as he pulled Rat aside.

"And me?" Rat asked

"Walk along with me, would you, son?" Cathcart asked. "Billy Bedford's brought word trouble's brewin' down the street. Got my deputy off to Weatherford just now. I wouldn't mind some company."

Rat nodded his understanding and accompanied the sheriff outside.

"Ain't been diggin' many posts lately, I don't suppose," Billy Bedford said as he handed Rat a shotgun.

"Nope," Rat answered with a grin. "Guess nowadays you've turned to other trades, too."

"Washin' glasses at the Lucky Lady," the boy explained as the sheriff started down the dusty street. "Got a fight buildin' tonight. Mr. Hull sent me for help."

"You found it," Cathcart declared. "Best you stand clear now, Billy. Leave it to us."

They were still a hundred yards short of the saloon when a pair of pistol shots punctured the night. There was a shout, followed by the sound of shattering glass. Sheriff Cathcart raced forward, and Rat stumbled along as well as he could. By the time the two of them reached the Lucky Lady, peace had already been restored.

"Anybody know him?" the sheriff asked as he knelt beside a the prone figure of a middle-aged man.

"Called himself Duncan," Eli Hull explained from behind the bar. "From Tennessee, I think."

"North o' there, I'd judge," Billy added. "Talked more like a Yank, and he told me he had a boy up Cincinnati ways."

"Was a fair fight, Sheriff," Mitchell Morris declared.

The sound of Mitch's voice pried Rat's eyes off the corpse stretched out on the floor. The fingers of the dead man's right hand even now gripped the handle of a Remington revolver. Mitch had slung a small pocket Colt on the gaming table alongside a pile of coins and bank notes.

"He's right," Hull agreed. "Other fellow's been jabberin' 'bout bein' cheated half the night. Twice invited Mitch here outside. Then he finally drew out a gun."

"Wasn't anything else I could do," Mitch testified.

"You others figure it so?" Cathcart asked a pair of shaken cardplayers.

"Was like he said," a bearded cowboy declared.

"Lucky the boy had that hideout gun," a younger wrangler added. "Been shot dead."

"This Ohio fellow didn't know you had a pistol, eh?" the sheriff asked. Mitch shook his head, and the lawman frowned. "Was you cheatin', boy?"

"Don't need to," Mitch explained. "I got luck."

"You sure had it this night," Cathcart declared. "Seems you were ready enough with that pistol. He fire first?"

"If he had, Mitch'd be dead," Hull answered.

"You wouldn't have me wait to take a bullet first, would you?" Mitch asked. "I was only defendin' myself."

"Well, I suppose that's how folks'll see it anyway," Cathcart grumbled. "I don't take to gamblers, Mitch, especially when they keep pistols ready. I won't charge you this time. But you keep your gun holstered in Thayerville. I'll not have killin' in my town!"

"I was only . . ." Mitch argued.

"You heard me, son!" the sheriff barked. "Now get along out o' here. We got a body to see tended."

"We were playin' stud," Mitch complained.

"You done your playin' this night," Cathcart announced. "Close down the bar, too, Eli. Been 'nough excitement."

Chapter Thirteen

Rat Hadley didn't speak to Mitch that night. No, Rat could think of nothing to say to his old friend. They had shared that violent afternoon on the Cimarron River and so many other bitter times. This new killing, though, was a foreign, unshared thing.

"Looks like you're not the only fellow 'round who can fill graves!" Mitch boasted the following afternoon. "Got me a man, too."

"Sure," Rat muttered. "Wasn't a thing I warmed to, though. Found no pleasure in it. Only pain."

"'Well, they shot you."

"Oh, it's more'n that, Mitch. Arms heal. Ain't been many nights I ain't seen that Curly Bob in my dreams. Cain't but barely recall what he looked like, but he's there just the same, a shadowy face grinnin' and shootin' me dead."

"Laugh at him, Rat! You got him 'fore he had his chance."

"Sure, I did. But I'm not sure it was a fair bargain I made. And now to hear you brag on it! Takes a hard heart to be a killer, I'd say."

"You just admitted to killin' a man yourself," Mitch complained.

"Sure, I did," Rat admitted. "But it wasn't in my mind. I didn't have much choice, what with Pop and all those passengers. Shoot, the Gardiner boy was right there! I kilt an outlaw, too, Mitch, and a wanted one at that. Still, if I could do it again I'm not sure . . ."

"Sure you are," Mitch argued. "And so would I. It was your job, Rat, just like it was mine to shoot that Ohio fellow."

"Yer job?" Rat cried.

"Gamblin's come to be my trade, Rat. I know my way around the games just fine, have for a long time. That's not enough to get a man along in years, though. He's got to know all the odds, scratch himself an edge. Sometimes that means sittin' on one side o' the table or another. Once in a while it means shavin' a card or two. But mostly you got to read the other fellow. And if you see him reachin' for a pistol, you best know it ahead o' time so you can be ready."

"Still, I'm not altogether sure I could pull a gun and shoot a man down like that," Rat mumbled. "Not up close so I could see his eyes and all."

"Maybe not, Rat. But then you always could stomach sour words better'n most men."

"More practice at it, I suppose."

"Me, when a man hints at me cheatin', my dander rises. Angry, I shoot a little quicker."

"Guess that's natural," Rat said gloomily. "Still, I never figured the two o' us'd be known in Thayerville for killin' other men."

"That's about the only common ground we got these days, though. Folks don't eye my shootin' quite the same as yours."

I don't myself, Rat told himself. The hard look in Mitch's eyes reflected an understanding of his friend's feelings. But then the two of them had few secrets.

"Enough 'bout that," Mitch said, managing a grin. "Tell me what brought you over last night. With the sheriff, I mean."

"Guess I was handy," Rat explained. "Little Billy Bedford come along to the barn dance and said trouble was brewin'. The sheriff asked me to come along, Henning Lewis bein' out o' town and all."

"Talk 'round town's that you been stayin' with him. Passin' time with Becky."

"She did a fair job o' tendin' me when I was laid up, Mitch. Ain't altogether bad lookin', you know."

"You had an eye for her ever since she was twelve."

"Never knew you to pass a chance for some female company," Rat said, blushing slightly. "Nor begrudge a friend some o' the same."

"You come a fair piece from Dodge City, Rat."

"No," Rat argued. "Just got myself home finally. Becky and me, we're comfortable."

"That all?" Mitch asked. "Don't sound too excitin'."

"Ain't you seen enough excitement o' late? Me, the dull ole things suit me just fine. Sunset walks and a kiss or two, talkin' 'bout dreams or ridin' out to the river."

"We used to do those things, Rat."

"Sure, but it's different tellin' Becky. I believe we could share some o' those dreams, Becky and me. She wants to."

"Plannin' on marryin' her, Rat?"

"Maybe. If the job with the Western holds out awhile and the market for horses gets some better. I got five-hundred dollars reward money for ole Curly Bob Clark, you know. And I put by some cash from cuttin' posts. Figure to buy myself some acres and run horses."

"Bet it'll work, Rat," Mitch said confidently. "Luck's been smilin' on you lately."

"Yeah, and I don't mind at all. How's she treatin' you, Mitch?"

"Keepin' me alive," Mitch answered. He then shuffled his feet and gazed off in the distance. Rat guesses the good cards were harder to come by these days.

"Mitch, you know I could use a partner if I got that ranch."

"You know I'm no good with animals," Mitch said, shaking his head and turning away. "Horses mostly stomp on my feet or toss me in cactus. 'Sides, Becky'll be your partner."

"You sure yer all right, Mitch?"

"Just as fine as I ever hoped to be," Mitch boasted. Instantly he revived his old grin, and the Morris charm seemed to flow as freely as Lucky Lady beer. "Not worryin' over me, I hope."

"No, you always do fine, don't you, Mitch?"

"Always," Mitch announced. "Every single time."

Rat wasn't reassured, though. That next week when he wasn't guarding the freight office, Rat accompanied Lem Cathcart around Thayerville.

"Ain't so different from ridin' guard on the stagecoach," Rat observed after a time. "Just got to have sharp eyes. That way you can see the trouble comin'."

"That's half o' it," Cathcart confided. "The rest is knowin' what to do when you spy the problem."

"Like Mitch said he did t'other night."

"Oh?"

"Said that fellow was edgin' closer and closer to drawin' his pistol. That let Mitch get ready."

"That's not at all what I mean," the sheriff objected. "You know, Rat, I've been a peace officer a few years now. More'n you've been alive. In all that time I've shot three men. Only two of 'em died."

"I already kilt two myself," Rat mumbled.

"First time I caught a man holdin' a shotgun on a bank teller in Jacksboro. If I'd called to him, he might've shot a dozen people. So I shot him twice. In the back. He never had a prayer."

"Was breakin' the law," Rat said, nodding. "Guess he didn't earn a chance."

"That's a truth, Rat," Cathcart delcared. "And if I'd risked my life when I didn't have to, I'd been the biggest kind of a fool."

"And the other one?"

"Just a boy," the lawman said, shaking his head sadly. "Drunk. Just back from makin' a cattle drive, and he had too much money in his pockets. Took to sprayin' the street with bullets, and I shot him."

"You had to protect folks."

"Found out he'd emptied his guns, Rat. If I'd talked to him some, I might've brought him in peaceful. It's a hard call sometimes, and I never altogether get that boy out o' my thoughts. Still, he broke the law. Was his choice to shoot up my town. I'm smarter now. I separate the drinkers from their guns early on, and I run the wild ones clear o' Thayerville."

"Got to be more to it."

"Is. I don't give 'em too big a piece o' myself for a target, and when I do have to shoot, I hit what I aim at."

"Me, too," Rat said with a sigh. "That's how I kilt Curly Bob. Just instinct more'n anything."

"And the first one?"

"Blind luck. Fellow charged up a hill at us, and I emptied my pistol at him and his friends. When the smoke cleared, he was dead. The whole time I was scared out o' my boots."

"Scared last time, too?"

"Yessir. But there were folks to protect, and wasn't nobody else to do it."

"That's the way it is for lawmen, son. Oh, killin' comes easy to some, but most find it hard. More so after they do it once or twice. But you always have good people dependin' on you, women and children and old people who can't do for themselves. So you find it's up to you."

Their conversation was cut short by the sound of glass shattering at the Lucky Lady.

"Sheriff!" Billy Bedford screamed as he raced out the swinging doors a step ahead of a flying chair.

"Lord, it's Hull's place again," Cathcart grumbled. "Come lend a hand, Rat. Trouble's at hand."

Rat nodded. And though he didn't have a shotgun this time, he was ready to do as ordered.

Sheriff Cathcart reached the saloon first. Rat arrived a moment later.

"It's that big fellow with the beard," Billy shouted, pointing to a giant of a man pressing a smaller figure's head against the hard wooden floor.

"Deal seconds to me, will you?" The giant hollered.

"Stop it!" Eli Hull pleaded. "You're tearin' up the place!"

"Place merits it," the big man replied. "I come to town for a fair game and find cheats here instead."

"I never saw any cheatin'!" a slim cowboy claimed. "Honest, mister, we play here all the time."

"I seen it!" a sandy-hair stranger decked out like a Ft. Worth banker exclaimed. "That boy's got slick fingers 'round the bottom o' yon deck."

"Oh, it's just losin' hands talkin'," the cowboy accused.

"Don't mean it ain't so," the giant bellowed. "Nobody's as lucky as this one!"

"Maybe so," Cathcart said, warily approaching the men. "Let him go though. This is for me to tend."

"I seen backwater towns afore," the big man grumbled. "Leave me to settle this."

"I said let him go," Cathcart demanded. The sheriff pulled a pistol and swung the barrel toward the bearded man's enormous belly.

"You cain't mean to shoot me for settlin' up with a cheat, Sheriff!"

"I'll do just that if you don't step away from him this instant."

The big man released his hold. Then, quick as lightning, the giant produced a knife and started for the sheriff. The lawman rammed the hammer back on his pistol, and the would-be assassin froze.

"Drop it!" Cathcart yelled.

Only now did Rat take in the whole scene. His racing heart left him short of breath, and the condition wasn't improved one bit when he recognized Mitch Morris's frightened face as the subject of the giant's attentions. A second later, though, Rat's mind cleared. The fancy-dressed gambler was fumbling with a valise. Out came a pistol, and the barrel swung toward Sheriff Cathcart.

"Sheriff, duck!" Rat yelled as he leaped toward the gunman and knocked the pistol aside. The gun fired, blowing a neat hole in the bar. Rat winced as the bigger man wrestled for control of the pistol. With a left arm only half-mended and the rest of him sore and softened by long days of recovery, Rat was no match for his opponent. Soon he was flung aside.

"Rat!" Mitch shouted as the fancy-dressed gambler pointed his gun down at Rat's helpless form. Then, from nowhere, Billy Bedford swung a brass spittoon across the gunman's skull, and the man collapsed in a heap.

"Try it, please," Sheriff Cathcart said, turning to the giant who was reaching for his discarded knife. "I'll send you to hell so fast you'll swear it was the devil himself drivin' the coach."

The big man backed away and raised his hands in surrender.

"He your partner?" Cathcart asked, pointing to the well-dressed figure stretched out on the floor.

"Just met him in Weatherford," the giant confessed. "Not partners exactly. He said we'd find easy pickin's here."

"Meanin' you'd call me for cheatin' and steal the pot," Mitch accused.

"Boy, I don't steal," the bearded Goliath claimed. "You was playin' with the deck all right. As to Hawkins there, well, who's to say what his game was. Close to got himself kilt, though."

"Both o' you," Mitch claimed as he picked up the knife. "Got a mind to see to it myself."

"That'd be a fool's play," Cathcart announced. "I'd be the one to do the shootin', Mitch."

"You saw him!" Mitch howled. "And th' other one's hurt Rat. Aimed a gun at you, too, Sheriff."

"Givin' me leave to shoot him," Cathcart explained. "Not you."

"Rat?" Mitch called.

"I'm all right," Rat grumbled as he got to his feet. "Owe Billy one, though."

"Back payment on more'n one service, Rat," young Bedford remarked. "Truth is, it felt just fine, swingin' that spittoon. Miss my ax, I suppose."

Rat grinned, then helped Sheriff Cathcart revive the fallen gambler.

"You got just five minutes to collect your wits and find your horses," the sheriff barked. "Then I'm haulin' you to the edge o' town and sendin' you on your way. Either o' you come back, I'll lock you up a year. Or maybe just shoot you 'tween the eyes. Don't know I could stand lookin' at you a year!"

A crowd had gathered, and they hooted their approval of the threat. The big man muttered to himself, stormed out onto Main Street, threw a leg over a mule, and headed on his way. The other fellow shook his head and moaned. A couple of cowboys tied him atop his horse and sent it headed south.

"Mitch, I don't want to see you for a time," Cathcart then declared. "Find somethin' else to occupy your time. Cards'll only bring on misfortune. Or worse. Could've been men killed here this day, and I won't have that. Not in my town."

"Yessir," Mitch said, backing away from the lawman.

"Too much drinkin's what it is," a woman cried. "Knives and guns and whiskey!"

"No, it's the cattle market," Cathcart argued. "Too many young hotheads with no work to occupy their time."

"Yeah," Rat agreed. "I know just how they feel."

"You got work now, though," Cathcart pointed out.

"For how long?" Rat asked. "Stage line's fine, but how long'll it last with the railroad runnin' twice as fast just south o' here?"

"You've done a fine job, Rat. Made yourself a reputation. Even if the Western went belly-up, you'd find work easy enough."

"Doin' what? Sloppin' hogs?"

"No, I was thinkin' more on the line o' becomin' a deputy sheriff."

"Where? Seems to me you got one already here in Thayerville."

"Henning Lewis's half the time off visitin' a particular friend over near

Albany. She's got herself a fine business there. Won't be long 'fore he heads there permanent. Meantime, I need myself somebody now and then. Pay you half o' Lewis's salary for takin' half his time."

"I got a job now, Sheriff."

"I spoke to Nate a week ago. He said they'd want you ridin' with the stage when you get better, but elsewise, you could deputy. Draw your regular wage, too. Might be you'll need the money by and by. For startin' up a family, for instance."

"Yeah," Rat said, grinning. "I'll give it some thought. It's a fine honor yer handin' me."

"I figure you earned the chance, son. Not a bad life, the law."

"No, sir," Rat said, pondering the matter. "Not bad at all."

Chapter Fourteen

Rat Hadley stood alongside Nate Parrott, greeting the westbound stage, when gunfire shattered the calm of a November afternoon.

"Best have a look," Parrott advised.

Rat nodded, grabbed his Winchester, and made his way down Main Street. He met Lem Cathcart and Henning Lewis fifteen yards short of the Lucky Lady.

"Got your rifle, I see," the sheriff noted.

"Yessir," Rat replied.

"Got a deputy's instincts, don't he, Lem?" Lewis asked. The deputy then led the way toward the Lucky Lady. Once in the doorway, he motioned the sheriff on. Rat followed Cathcart. Inside, powder smoke hung in the acrid air. There was also an odor of death. A solitary cowboy was slumped across a gaming table in the saloon's back corner. Nearby Mitch Morris stood, pocket Colt pistol in hand.

"Done it again, eh?" Cathcart called angrily.

"Th'other fellow reached first," Mitch explained. "Was him or me, Sheriff."

"That right?" Cathcart asked a huddle of onlookers.

"Happened real fast," one cowboy answered.

The others seemed equally uncertain.

"Eli, what happened here?" Cathcart asked angrily.

Hull shrugged, but Billy Bedford stepped out from behind the bar and approached the sheriff glumly.

"Was like before," the boy declared. "Jeb there," Billy added, pointing to the slain card player, "thought Mitch was cheatin'. They argued a bit. Then the shootin' happened."

"He had a gun, too," Mitch said, pointing to a pistol resting on the floor below the cowboy's lifeless fingers.

"Best we take him along to the jail house," Lewis suggested. "Have a regular trial."

"Nothin's clear," Cathcart grumbled. "I'll take your Colt, Mitch. And I want you clear o' town this day."

"Sheriff . . ." Mitch began.

"Gone!" Cathcart shouted. "I warned you last time. Ought to see you hung. But that'd be poor return to John and Mary for long years o' good service to this town."

"I was only defendin' myself," Mitch argued.

Cathcart stepped over and grasped Mitch by his shoulders. The sheriff shook the young killer angrily, then slung him against the wall of the saloon. Cathcart tossed the small Colt to Lewis, then pointed Mitch toward the door.

"Go!" the sheriff shouted. This time Mitch staggered to the door and made his exit.

"Sheriff, he only . . ." Rat started to argue. An angry stare hushed Rat. He, too, left the saloon.

"Where do I go?" Mitch cried, turning toward Rat. "I never knew anywhere else as home."

"I don't know," Rat answered. "Somewhere, though, 'cause Sheriff Cathcart's in a fine fever."

Mitch nodded and started toward the livery.

"Wasn't anything else I could do," he called to Rat. "Not anything!"

Rat didn't reply. He felt numb, empty, and not a little betrayed. Something was slipping away. And he was alone.

"Leave him to go his way," Sheriff Cathcart said from the door of the saloon. "Best be shed o' him, son."

"How can you say that?" Rat asked. "He's my best friend."

"He's a no-account," Cathcart declared. "And a killer. He's sure to come to a bad end and drag others along with him."

A great chill took possession of Rat. The rifle in his hands seemed like ice. He turned and hurried back to the stage office.

"Rat?" Nate Parrott called when the young guard slammed the Winchester down on the counter.

"I got to ride a bit," Rat told Parrott. "Be gone a day or two."

"You all right?"

"I don't know," Rat confessed. "I just need some time to think over things."

"Your horse's in the ready corral. I'll get him saddled."

"I can tend it myself," Rat barked. And with that said, Rat made his way to the corral.

As always when Rat Hadley needed to think, he sought the open country alongside the Brazos. That river always seemed capable of washing away pain and confusion, of reviving hope and promise. He rode five miles along the winding river before stopping. He was frozen by the sight of the towering white oak on the far bank.

Come a long ways, it seems, to wind up here, Rat thought. *Ole Boswell must've felt the same way.*

Rat then splashed across the shallows and dismounted. After securing his horse to the white oak, he removed the saddle and threw a blanket on the rocky ground. There he passed the cold, heartless afternoon and the longer empty night.

Morning found him watching the sun creep over the far hills. His stomach rumbled with hunger, and he drew a length of line from his saddlebags, fastened a hook, and snared a cricket for bait. In no time he managed to snag a plump bass. He built a small fire and cooked the fish trail style, on a green stick over glowing coals.

Rat passed the balance of the morning drifting here and there across the low hills. So many memories lurked in that place. Shadows he thought to have escaped returned to torment him.

Mitch arrived a little after midday.

"Asked for you in town," Mitch explained. "Parrott said you went ridin'. Somehow I knew you'd be up here."

"Where else?" Rat asked.

"Brought a rifle. Thought maybe we could scare up a deer like in the old days."

"Not had yer fill o' killin' things?" Rat asked accusingly.

"Maybe, but a man's got to survive. He does things to get through one day to the next."

"Wonder if it's altogether worth it," Rat grumbled.

"Wouldn't you fight a bit for your dream, Rat? For that horse ranch you figure to have with Becky?"

"I'm not sure I'd kill to get it," Rat replied. "That sours everything."

"Maybe so," Mitch admitted. "Right now, though, I got the urge to hunt these hills with my best friend. Like we used to when the two o' us together couldn't muster a chin whisker."

"For old times then," Rat agreed.

"Sure, for old times' sake."

The hunt worked like a balm, salving Rat's hurts. There was something about stalking deer across those empty, rocky ridges to draw a man back to his beginnings. Mitch had been right about that. Five years of hurt seemed to fade as warmer, better memories flooded Rat's mind. And when they finally located a pair of bucks near a small pond, Mitch passed the rifle to Rat.

"Yer shot," Rat argued.

"I never could hit anything with a rifle," Mitch argued. "You found 'em. Drop us one so we don't starve."

Rat nodded sadly, then cradled the rifle and fixed his sights on the larger of the bucks. It was a proud-looking creature with a fair set of antlers. Rat's left arm ached some, and a flash of pain followed the rifle's discharge. The buck fell instantly, though, and the hurt passed.

"Same ole Rat!" Mitch yelled as the other deer scattered. "Crack shot!"

"Let's get about the butcherin'," Rat muttered. "It's not goin' to stay light forever, you know."

"No, dark comes early this time o' year," Mitch agreed. "And with it winter's chill."

The sun was nesting on the western horizon when the two old friends returned to their camp with the venison. The weight of the meat was almost too much for them, and Rat regretted not taking a horse along. His bad arm felt as if it would pop out of its socket, and the rest of him was just plain exhausted. Mitch knew it, and he started making the fire.

"Turnin' cold," Mitch observed as he scraped the handle of his knife across a length of flint to spark a pile of dry brush. "November's here, and winter's certain to follow."

"Yeah," Rat agreed. "Hard times comin'."

It was later, while thick venison steaks crackled over the fire, that Mitch began recounting half-forgotten adventures they'd shared as boys. There were days spent swimming in the river or chasing mustangs, bedeviling farmers or raiding neighbors.

"Strange how things've turned," Mitch said sadly. "I'd give most anything to be fourteen again, to start it all over."

"Not me," Rat grumbled. "I been through my hard times."

"And mine's just beginnin'," Mitch said, sighing.

"It'll all die down in a bit," Rat argued. "Sheriff Cathcart won't hold a grudge, Mitch. In a month or so he won't mind you comin' home, even playin' cards at the Lucky Lady. It's the killin' he hates. And the notion his town's gone sour."

"A month?" Mitch said, laughing to himself as he drew a charred steak off the fire. "Might not be alive in a month."

"What?"

"I been the worst kind o' fool, Rat," Mitch confessed as he passed the steak to his friend. "Went down to Weatherford. They got hard men there. I played cards with a pair o' them. I figured I could hold my own, but they had all the luck. I tried everything, even shaved a card or two. I had to bring the chips back my way. It was like before, at the Double L, only I couldn't shoot my way out o' trouble."

"I don't understand."

"Rat, those fellows weren't lyin'. I wasn't playing' 'em square. Both times they had me caught and knew it. Pure luck saved me. They tried to settle things with pistols, and I was ready."

"And at Weatherford?"

"Didn't work that way. Two men called my game. Another had a shotgun on my back. I lost everything. My money, and maybe my hide, too, if I don't come up with what I owe 'em."

"You owe them money?"

"I used a marker in the game, Rat. I had to get my losin's back. Only I went on losin'."

"How much do you owe?"

"Two-hundred dollars."

"Lord, Mitch!" Rat exclaimed. "That's a fortune."

"For some," Mitch confessed. "Me, I won that much before, and I will again once luck turns my way. All I need's time."

"Two-hundred dollars, though! Where'll you get it? Do yer folks have that kind o' cash?"

"No, nor would they lend it to me," Mitch said, frowning. "Ma says cards's the devil's tools. You recall that, don't you? Scolded us plenty when she caught us havin' a game o' poker."

"They'd understand if you went to 'em," Rat declared. "Yer their boy, after all. They'd help you. They think yer the best man ever set foot on the earth."

"We know better, of course. And if I told them, what pain would that cause?"

"But what else'll you . . ."

"Why do you figure I come up here, Rat?"

"What?"

"The reward money. Five-hundred dollars."

"That's for my ranch, Mitch."

"I wouldn't need it all," Mitch said, frowning. "Look, Rat, I'd have to have two hundred to get even and another fifty for a stake. I could start fresh."

"That's my future, Mitch. It's for Becky. It's a house, land, a good stud. I need it."

"Rat, it's only blind luck brought you that money. You said yourself you didn't know it was Curly Bob Clark set out after you, and you didn't mean to kill him. Luck run your way for once. And it sure as hell's turned its eyes from me."

"It's a lot to ask, Mitch," Rat muttered. "More'n a man ought to, I'm thinkin'."

"More'n riskin' your life ridin' out to see a friend when a shotgun-totin' varmint threatened to kill you? More'n riskin' your neck to save somebody in pain? More'n takin' in a boy, sharin' your home, family, everything? We been brothers, Rat. I give you everything a man can give. I ain't asked much in return. Not in my whole life."

"Nor've I," Rat replied.

"It's my life, Rat. Now it's me needs help, and I come to you. There's nobody else."

Rat stared hard into the eyes of his old friend. Desperation lurked in those tormented eyes. Rat recognized the expression. It drew them both back to another time and place. The scars on Rat's back seemed to eat into his soul, and the specter of ole man Plank's vicious face seemed to dance in the flames of the campfire.

"I got the money locked up in the company safe," Rat explained. "We'll go into town tomorrow and fetch it."

"You've saved my life," Mitch said, clasping Rat's hand.

"Returnin' a favor," Rat answered. "Payin' a debt."

"Wasn't ever a debt," Mitch argued. "We been bonded, the two o' us, for a long time. It's just another trial shared."

Rat nodded. *It's the last one shared,* he told himself. For things had changed between them.

They passed the chill night in an uneasy silence. Once venison steaks would have brought warming contentment. Now there was only a cold void, together with a sense that something valuable had been lost.

Next morning Rat led the way into Thayerville. He paused but a few minutes at the Cathcart place to deliver the deerhide full of fresh venison. Then he galloped along to the Western Stage Line office.

"Well, what do you know?" Nate Parrott cried when Rat entered the office. "Figured you for a week's ridin' easy."

"I need to draw some money from the safe," Rat explained.

"Set your mind on that ranch, have you? Well, we'll miss you, son. But a man's bound to make himself a fresh beginnin' now and then."

"I only need half," Rat added. "And I won't be goin' anyplace. Truth is, I'll be ready to ride guard again tomorrow."

"You sure?" Parrott asked.

"I'm sure," Rat answered.

"Well, you go ahead and draw what you need from the safe. You know how. That packet's still got your name on her. Be easy enough to find."

Rat nodded and went about it. He gazed nervously at Mitch's face in the side window. And twice he misdialed the combination. In truth Rat didn't want to part with the money, forestall his own dream. In the end, though, he counted off the bank notes and took them to Mitch Morris.

"They got a lot o' trust in you, Rat," Mitch observed when they met outside. "Must be plenty o' money passes through this office."

"Enough," Rat replied, passing over the money. "It's a fine thing for somebody to hold you in esteem, you know. Might be you ought to consider such work yerself."

"Part o' me wants to," Mitch confessed. "But I got the itch to deal cards. It'd be a hard fork to take in the road after knowin' what it's like to sleep in silk sheets and wear fancy clothes, have soft shoulders to hold come nightfall, and spend what I like for what I want."

"It's a mirage, that life," Rat argued. "Nothin' easy lasts more'n a moment. Life's dark and hard and bitter cold."

"Sure it is," Mitch said, folding the bills and stuffing them in his pocket. "Less luck's with you. Be a time 'fore we see each other again, Rat. You watch out for yourself."

"You, too, Mitch," Rat said, clasping his old friend's hand. And yet as they parted, there was none of the old warmth left behind.

Chapter Fifteen

Rat tended his horse before returning to the Cathcart house. Earlier, when he'd dropped off the venison, he'd hardly spoken a word. Now he found himself greeted by anxious eyes.

"Pa won't favor you ridin' with Mitch Morris," Busby muttered as he held the door open. "He don't like Mitch much."

"I know," Rat replied.

"We worried about you," Becky broke in. "You might let people know when you ride off into the hills."

"Didn't figure I was a boy like Buzz, needin' permission to do a little huntin'," Rat barked. "I been a long time growed up, Becky. A long time."

"And you've been a considerable time part o' this family," she argued. "I think we're owed some consideration in return for our attentions."

"Brought you a deer," Rat countered. "If it's not enough, maybe I'd better pack up my gear and move back over to Pop's place. Might be best.

I'll be ridin' to Albany on the stage tomorrow mornin' anyhow."

"I thought Pa . . ."

"Thought what?" Rat asked. "That I give up my job? Man's got to earn his way, you know."

"What about the ranch?" she cried. "You've got the reward money now. I was hopin' maybe the two o' us might ride out and look around some."

"Spoke to a preacher, too, I'll wager," Rat grumbled. "Don't you think I got some say in my life?"

"Of course," she said sourly. "It's only . . ."

"We done some dreamin'," Rat told her. "Nothin' more. Now I'm mended, it's time I was about my business."

"Rat . . ."

"You sayin' I made promises, Becky? Did I pledge myself?"

"No," she said, dropping her eyes to the floor. "But I thought we shared some feelin's."

"We do," he confessed. "But I forgot some matters. Best get 'em tended 'fore I do any more dreamin'."

She gazed with hurt eyes, and Rat wanted to draw her to him, stroke her soft cheeks and comfort her with kinder words. But come daybreak he'd still climb atop the westbound, and he'd be riding beside Pop Palmer for weeks, maybe years. It would be cruel to promise otherwise, and unfair to hint of a settled life without the cash money to make it so.

"You ought to take her for a walk," Busby scolded when they were alone in the little side room later. "She thinks Pa told you to keep some distance. Or else you've soured on her. Haven't, have you?"

"No, it isn't her, nor her pa, neither," Rat replied. "It's me. Seems like the ground beneath my feet's slippin' away, and I got nothin' to hold onto."

"You got us. Becky especially."

"Ain't enough just now," Rat told the boy. Busby's eyes, as Becky's had earlier, searched for an explanation that Rat couldn't provide. He didn't understand things himself. Only time could sort it all out, and Rat hoped he would have that time.

Next morning he climbed atop the westbound coach. Where before he had felt oddly comfortable up there, Winchester in hand, he now found the rifle's touch cold and foreign.

"Feels good, havin' you back," Pop said when he maneuvered his considerable girth onto the hard wooden bench beside Rat. "Brought you some ham and biscuits for later. And a touch o' spirits, too, in case the arm takes to hurtin'."

Pop drew out a corked bottle, and Rat nodded. They were only two miles out of Thayerville when he took his first sip.

"Knew you were hurryin' it," Pop grumbled. "I had a broke arm myself once. Bouncin' around atop a stagecoach ain't no way to get it mended."

"I'm mended," Rat growled. "Leastwise my arm is."

"Well, a man couldn't tell it by yer humor."

"Sorry, Pop," Rat said, returning the bottle. "I got no call to bark at everybody. I just got some figurin' to do, and it ain't gettin' itself done."

"Had a fight with the sheriff's gal?"

"Not a fight," Rat muttered. "Shoot, it ain't her, neither, Pop. It's me. I got myself twisted round, and I can't seem to find my way. It's like huntin' a trail and findin' a river what ain't got fords."

"Well, nobody else's goin' to get you down that road," Pop observed. "I had a crossroads myself once upon a time, though. It's when I found my Varina."

"Had any regrets?"

"Well, I wouldn't make much of a trail cowboy, Rat. And there's comfort at night, feelin' her close, listenin' to the little ones stirrin'. Cain't say I never looked back, but it was the right trail for me."

"And me?"

"I ain't much for givin' out advice," the driver declared. "But Becky's a mighty sensible gal. A man could make a worse bargain."

"Yeah, I guess he could," Rat said thoughtfully.

"Now I've said what I know to that business," Pop remarked. "Let me tell you 'bout that scamp Tyler."

Pop rattled off one tale after another of his boys and little Velma, and the miles rolled along beneath the wheels of the coach. Except for a brief stop to satisfy nature's demands and to give the horses a drink, the stage plodded its way west without a hitch.

Rat found his uneasiness passing. By and by he settled into the swaying rhythm of the coach. His eyes kept watch on the adjacent rocks and hills, but not so much as a shadow attracted his attention. They rolled into Albany ahead of schedule, and Rat climbed down and bid the passengers farewell.

The return trip started out the same way. But not five miles out of Albany Rat spotted a shadowing horseman.

"Look yonder," Pop called, pointing to a slender rider poised on the crest of a low hill just ahead.

"One behind us, too," Rat explained. "Could be trouble."

"More likely out o' work cowboys," Pop said nervously. "Not masked."

Rat saw it was true, but most cowboys would offer a friendly wave to a passing coach. These riders kept themselves to the shadows, and once the Western passed, the second rider galloped over and joined the other trailing horseman.

"Figure another ambush?" Pop asked.

"It's the best way to do it," Rat answered. "Plenty o' narrow spots in the rocks up ahead. And we got a stop for water scheduled, too. They'd know that, I suppose."

"Well, if they suppose I'll pull this coach to a halt with men followin' along behind, they got another think comin'. My ma didn't raise herself any idiots, and my kids expect more o' their pop."

"Maybe I should throw a shot their way," Rat suggested.

"Better to save the lead," Pop advised. "Anyhow, they could be peaceable characters after all."

"You don't believe that," Rat muttered.

"No," Pop confessed. "But it'd be a shame to put a hole in a poor cowboy just the same."

Rat nodded, but he continued to eye the stalking strangers as they appeared ghostlike in and out of the dusty cloud thrown up by the coach's churning wheels.

Bit by bit the coach pulled ahead of its pursuers. Rat expected an ambush in the hills south of the Brazos, but none came. It made no sense to string out a raid like this!

"Ain't so dumb," Pop pointed out when he slowed the stage as they splashed across a rocky creek. "Look to the horses. They got themselves lathered proper. Cain't drive 'em hard forever."

"Nor ourselves," Rat added. "Got any notions?"

"There's a bend in the trail just ahead. Water for the horses, and good cover, too. We can pull off, rest a bit, and see what those dust-eaters got in mind."

Rat nodded his agreement, and Pop eased the pace.

"We'll be stoppin' just ahead, folks!" Pop yelled to the passengers. "We picked ourselves up some company, though. Keep a wary eye out for trouble."

"That's your job!" an elderly woman remarked.

"We'll do what we can," Pop promised. "But you folks watch yerselves just the same."

There was a good deal of grumbling below, but Rat made little sense of it. Between the whining of the axles and the pounding of the hooves, he was lucky to hear Pop half the time.

"That's the place yonder!" Pop said, motioning to the turn in the trail just ahead. He then slowed the horses to a walk and allowed them to splash into the shallows of a stream before halting.

"See anything?" Pop called.

"Not a sign," Rat answered as he crawled between the trunks and boxes tied atop the coach. He burrowed his way into the middle of them and swung the Winchester to bear on the trail behind them. The trailing riders had vanished, and no sign of trouble appeared elsewhere.

"Maybe it *was* just cowboys," Pop said as he clambered down from his driver's bench and opened the door of the coach. He helped down the old woman, then beckoned the other two passengers out as well. One was a Ft. Worth cattle buyer named Johnson who traveled the coach regularly. The other was a Presbyterian preacher returning from an Albany wedding.

"You staying atop there to keep watch?" Johnson asked as he stepped out onto the rocky ground.

"Yessir," Rat answered. "We had some company a ways back."

"Saw 'em," the cattle buyer remarked. "Seen one of 'em before."

"Oh?" Rat asked.

"Rode with the Oxenbergs."

Rat nodded his understanding. Nate Parrott had spoken of the Oxenberg brothers and their habit of raiding coaches and freight wagons along the Clear Fork of the Brazos. There was something else about them, too. Lem Cathcart had mentioned how Efrem Plank had taken up with that bunch. Ef knew the country ahead close to as well as Rat Hadley did.

"They hit us before along here," Pop said gruffly. "Let's hurry ourselves, folks. I wouldn't care to meet up with trouble."

"Boy, you yell out if you see anything!" Johnson urged when Pop escorted the other passengers down the creek a ways. "I've got a fair measure o' cash on my person, and there are people in Albany knew it. I'm a good shot with a pistol, though."

"May need to be," Rat replied. "But there's open country ahead o' us. We get through these hills, and we can hold our own."

Johnson nodded, then trotted off to tend to his needs. A quarter hour later Pop announced the horses refreshed, and the passengers hurried back inside the coach. Palmer returned to his place, and the stage resumed its journey.

Rat began to believe the worry was all for naught. The riders had failed to reappear, and they hadn't really threatened the coach anyway. But as Pop Palmer turned the stage northward and began to thread his way through the last of the low hills, a pair of rifle shots greeted them from the brush just ahead.

"Yah!" Pop yelled, lashing the horses into extra efforts. "Yah!"

What did you expect? Rat asked himself as he fired his Winchester at the white wisps of powder smoke. *Fightin's what you were hired for!*

The marksmen seemed to be aiming at the horses, hoping to halt the coach. But Pop got the team moving faster than the outlaws anticipated, and the shots mostly peppered the back of the coach. One did splinter the preacher's oaken trunk, but in the end the real danger appeared from other quarters.

To being with, the two young riders reappeared on Rat's left. Another pair charged from the right, and three others blocked the trail ahead. Not a one of them had a weapon to match the Winchester's range, though, and to use their handguns they had to close with the coach. Even an experienced hand had trouble hitting a target as he bounced along in the saddle, and none of the raiders seemed much past boyhood.

Johnson, firing from the coach window, had the edge. The first outlaw to pull even with the stage found that out. A single bullet shattered the raider's jaw, and he fell with a shriek onto the dusty trail. Rat's rifle discouraged the pair closing in from the right flank. As for the three ahead, they opened up a withering fire.

"Rat!" Pop Palmer cried as bullets tore into the coach and threatened the horses.

Rat turned his rifle and waited an instant as the sights filled with the forehead of a masked outlaw. Rat squeezed his trigger, and had not the bandit's horse turned, there would have been one less member of the Oxenberg gang. As it was, the bullet struck the right-hand rider instead, but far from fatally. Rat's second shot cut the middle rider's reins and sent him on a wild ride atop his frantic mount. The remaining gunman fired a final shot before fleeing as well.

"Get us through, Pop!" Rat urged as he fired at the retiring outlaws. "Keep 'em at it!"

"I don't need any encouragement," Pop answered as he whipped the horses onward. "Those fool raiders went and broke my whiskey bottle!"

Rat couldn't help laughing as the driver held up a fragment of glass. It could as well have been Pop's fat jowls that took that bullet!

The Oxenbergs pursued the stage close to four more miles, but the shooting was from long range, and Rat had no more luck than did the raiders. Bullets flew back and forth, but they found only dust, rock, or prickly pear for targets. Ten miles shy of Thayerville the gang retired, leaving Rat a chance to wipe his forehead and clear the dust from his throat.

"You folks all right down below?" Pop called to the passengers.

"Not a hole in any of us," the preacher shouted. "Praise the good Lord for delivering us from our trials."

"Praise Rat Hadley's more like it," Pop objected. "You sure broke up that bunch up ahead!"

"Was lucky this time," Rat muttered. "They had us cold, Pop, if they'd known how to shoot."

"Just boys's all, Rat," the driver said, shaking his head. "Boys that ought to be cowboyin' if times weren't so bad. If the Oxenbergs'd been up front, we'd known it. Likely they were back on that hill."

"Or maybe it wasn't them at all," Rat suggested. "I didn't spy Efrem Plank, and I hear he rides with 'em now."

"You seen Ef lately?"

"No," Rat confessed.

"Didn't think so, Rat, 'cause that one you sent off on his horse had the look of a Plank to me."

"Yeah?"

"I'd figure them to come back at us, too."

"Would seem likely," Rat admitted.

When the coach pulled to a stop at the Western office, Nate Parrott greeted them with a grin.

"You're early, Pop!" Parrott called.

"Had some encouragement," Pop noted, pointing to the bullet holes in the side of the coach. Two of the horses bled from holes in their sides, too, and Parrott's smile faded quickly.

"Was the Oxenberg bunch," Johnson announced to the crowd that was collecting. "I dropped one of 'em, and the guard there hit a couple more. Kept 'em occupied a little while."

"Well, Rat, not much of a welcome back for you, was it?" Parrott asked.

"Glad he was along, though," Palmer commented. "He and that Winchester know their business."

Rat climbed down to the cheers of a fair-sized crowd. Tyler and Hollis Palmer shook his hand, and Billy Bedford grinned in admiration. Then Rat's eyes spied Becky Cathcart. He found only grave concern in her eyes.

"Let's make some room now," Sheriff Cathcart bellowed, and the people cleared the way. "I need to visit a moment with you folks. I could use a description of the raiders."

Rat nodded and motioned Pop and the passengers inside the office. Johnson and the preacher gave sketchy descriptions of the outlaws. The old woman pronounced them as young and left that to suffice.

"Efrem Plank was among 'em," Pop Palmer added. "And there was a youngster used to work at the livery, called himself Gill."

"Ted Gill," Parrott muttered. "He tended horses for me last year."

"You add anything, Rat?" the sheriff asked.

"I was pretty busy," Rat explained. "And I don't know much o' anybody hereabouts anymore."

"Well, I'll bring by some posters. You might match a face if it's before you again."

"Might," Rat agreed. "Mostly they looked young, though. And they didn't appear to know the trade."

"I told you they were youngsters, Sheriff," the woman barked. "Told you!"

"Yes'm," Cathcart answered with a bemused grin. "I made note o' it, too."

Johnson drew the sheriff aside then, and Rat seized the opportunity to make his escape. His hands still held the Winchester, seemed glued to the gun, in fact. He felt that need to wash away the dust and the powder smoke and the scent of death from his hide. And the memory, too, if that were possible.

Chapter Sixteen

Rat rode guard four days a week thereafter, making the swing to Albany Tuesdays and Fridays, then coming back to Thayerville each Wednesday and Saturday. Each time he and Pop Palmer set out across the empty, rock-studded countryside, Rat expected the Oxenbergs to strike. But the outlaws devoted their attentions elsewhere. Winter came and went peacefully.

Come spring Rat Hadley spent his off days as occasional deputy sheriff of Thayerville. It wasn't particularly hard work, and he enjoyed accompanying Lem Cathcart on evening rounds.

"Helps to have a man to watch your back," the sheriff explained as they made their way up Front Street. "Not much to hazard a man in Thayerville, but there's always the odd chance o' comin' across bad fortune. A peace officer can't always make friends, and there are those who hold the law against him personal. Those who'd break it as well. So you see, two pair o' eyes beat one most every time."

The sheriff passed on other lessons, mostly as concerned watching and listening, knowing when to act and when to wait. Rat knew well the sounds of the range, the scents of the wild mustangs and longhorn cattle that roamed there. Town noises were a different thing, and the shelter to be found in doorways or behind woodpiles were fresh discoveries.

"If a lawman's to see his grandchildren reared, he's got to know all these things," Cathcart declared. And Rat took it as gospel, coming as it did from a man who had become a second father.

The belonging Rat Hadley had found with the Cathcarts warmed him when the nights were cold and bitter. He found new reasons to smile daily. Among the town's boys he was a sort of hero, and as he shared stories of his days driving cattle or chasing ponies, he read the same admiration in the eyes of Randy and Vesty Plank and the Palmer boys that he had found gazing at Busby Cathcart or Billy Bedford. More and more their elders tipped hats or spoke cheerful greetings to a man who not long before had been looked upon as scarcely better than horse leavings.

Respect came more begrudgingly from other quarters, though. Strangers saw him only as a scrawny excuse for a deputy, and cowboys just in off the range resented the prosperity Rat enjoyed in hard times.

"Best to step aside from trouble," Cathcart advised when two Circle H cowboys blocked the walkway in front of the bank.

"Ain't got much talent for that," Rat argued.

"Can't fight the whole world, son."

"Cain't?" Rat asked. "Been doin' it a long time."

In truth, though, he was learning to walk with an easier step. That was mostly Becky's doing. She had a way of softening life, sprinkling each day with a bit of laughter. She eased him into civilized things, like Christmas sing-songs or sledding with the children. And when she suggested he escort her to the spring fiesta, he naturally agreed.

"You'll need some new clothes," she then told him. "Shoes, too."

"Bet you spend a week's salary gettin' outfitted proper," Buzz said, laughing.

"More likely a month's," Rat replied, sighing.

In the end, though, he deemed it worth the cost for the look on Becky's face when he led her onto Main Street.

"Well, folks, we best lock up the womenfolk!" John Morris cried. "Mr. Erastus Hadley's got himself on the prowl."

"Erastus?" Billy Bedford asked. "That yer real name, Rat?"

"One I's born with," Rat confessed. "Shed it early on, though."

"Don't blame you," Billy said, stepping back quickly to avoid Rat's grasp.

"I've got to help Ma ready the food tables," Becky said, halting him from pursuing the taunting youngster. "Can I trust you to stay clear o' trouble for a bit?"

"Maybe," Rat answered. "I am a deputy sheriff nowadays, you know."

"Well, keep that in mind," she suggested.

He flashed her a smile, then released her hand. As she hurried to help the other women set out platters of food on a series of tables along the south side of Main Street, Rat trotted over to where the Plank youngsters were setting off firecrackers. Rat thought it fortunate the street had been cleared of horses, for surely there would have been a stampede or two. In short order Vesty managed to send two dogs fleeing for their lives, and Randy fired a bottle rocket through the lobby of the hotel, scattering visitors in every direction.

"Sure be a shame to arrest a couple o' fine upstandin' citizens like yerselves," Rat told the youngsters.

"Be a shame to set yer boots on fire, too," Vesty warned.

Rat thereupon grabbed the boys by their suspenders and tossed them in a nearby trough. Grateful townspeople cheered.

Rat likewise managed to rescue the town from a band of pea-shooting outlaws led by Busby Cathcart.

"Sheriff might have words for you over such behavior," Rat warned.

"More'n words, I expect," Buzz answered. "Guess maybe we can turn to other business for a time, eh?"

His companions agreed whole-heartedly, and Rat chased the bunch of them along down the street.

By the time Becky finished her duties, Rat had tired of riding herd on Thayerville's younger population. He was just twenty himself, after all, so he excused himself and led Becky toward the mercantile. The street there was devoted to games of every sort, and they quickly joined in the fun. Becky managed to dunk his head under while he was bobbing for apples, and they stumbled in a hopeless tangle of spindly legs during a three-legged race.

"Guess it's not our day," Rat grumbled.

"I wouldn't say so," Becky replied with a grin. She rested her head on his chest a moment, and he brushed hair out of her eyes.

"Guess I've made a mess o' myself," she lamented.

"I never knew you prettier," he argued. "Nor felt stronger."

She smiled, then threw her arms around his neck and drew him close.

"Becky, folks's lookin'," he objected.

"Let 'em," she said, kissing his forehead. "Can't be a secret, our feelin's."

"Don't suppose so," Rat admitted, returning the kiss. "But I do think we ought to get out o' this street and let people get back to their business."

She gazed up at the crowd of pointing children and laughed. Rat stood, then helped her to her feet. Together they hurried along to where an arcade had been built. Among the fiesta booths were all sorts of tossing games. Rat disdained them. When they reached a target range, though, Henning Lewis shouted.

"Here's Rat Hadley!" the deputy called. "Best shot in town by most accounts. Care to take a shot, Rat? Prize is a plump turkey fit for a Sunday kettle. Becky there can bake it up perfect."

"I don't think so," Rat declined. "I don't like turkey."

"I do," Becky declared. "Go ahead and have a try, Rat."

"Yeah, Rat!" Tyler Palmer urged. "Henning took his turn and only hit seven targets."

"He's right," Lewis admitted. "Defend the honor of Thayerville, Rat. Some fellow off the Circle H hit eight."

"Go ahead, Rat," others cried. "Hit 'em all."

Rat turned to leave, but hands drew him back. Becky's eyes pleaded.

"Show 'em who you are, Rat," she whispered.

Who I am? he asked himself. *What did shooting a rifle have to do with that?* Nevertheless he picked up one of the Winchesters lying on a counter and examined it carefully. Ten playing cards were set up like targets fifty feet away, and he was to take one shot at each.

Rat rested the rifle lightly in his hands. It felt familiar, too familiar. Lately rifles and pistols were becoming tools, no different than axes used to fell trees. Except bullets tore through flesh and toppled men.

"Ten shots," Lewis declared, waving the onlookers back. Rat raised the gun and took aim. He then aimed at the first target and fired. The shot nicked the lower left corner of a red deuce. The gun pulled that way, and Rat adjusted his aim thereafter. In short order he riddled one card after another. When he got to the final target, an angry-faced black king, his bullet obliterated the whole head.

"I think he got 'em all," Tyler yelled.

Henning Lewis accepted the smoking rifle, then raced to check the score. He returned with the ten peppered cards and posted Rat's score.

"Take some doin' to top that!" Tyler Palmer shouted.

"It's hardly fair," a Circle H cowboy grumbled. "Everybody knows he rides guard for the Western Stage. It's his trade, shootin'."

"Yours's ropin'," Randy Plank noted. "Seems like you were tossin' a lariat down the ways, weren't you?"

The cowboy muttered to himself and left. Rat took Becky's arm and led her along the street a ways.

"There's truth in what he said," Rat told her.

"You don't do any more shootin' than range cowboys do," she argued. "Anyway, we've been here better'n an hour and we haven't joined the dancin'. Care to, Mr. Hadley?"

"Delighted, Miss Cathcart," he replied.

In truth, Rat never had been much of a dancer. He was no match for the wild-swinging cowboys or the more polished town boys. Becky got him through the steps, though, and at least they didn't fall down as before.

"Care to sit a bit?" Rat asked after their third dance.

"Sure," she agreed. "Let's find a chicken leg and some corn to gnaw. I'm starved."

It was while they were making their way to the food tables that Coley Hanks stepped in the way.

"Not leavin' the dancin' so soon, are you?" young Hanks asked. "Shoot, Becky, I was on my way to ask you to be my partner. After gettin' your feet trampled by Hadley here, I figured you to deserve somethin' better."

"We're on our way to get some food," Becky explained. "Maybe another time."

"Now," Hanks objected. He grabbed Becky's hand and turned toward the dancing. Rat pried the cowboy's fingers loose and stepped between him and Becky.

"You heard her," Rat said, managing a grin. "Now, if you'll excuse us . . ."

"Get out o' the way, Hadley!" Hanks shouted, angrily reaching for Rat's shoulders. Rat stepped back and allowed the cowboy to fall.

"You've had yerself a gulletful o' corn, Coley," Rat barked. "Best take a walk."

"Oh?" Hanks growled as he picked himself up.

"You can't fight him, Coley," another cowboy advised. "He's a deputy sheriff nowadays."

"That right?" Hanks asked. "You goin' to lock me in the jail house? Just who'd you be to tell anybody what to do or where to go? You crawled 'round half this country lookin' for work! Shoot, we all know your own ma turned you out when she skedaddled for Austin. You'd starved if my grandpa hadn't spoken up for you!"

Rat's face reddened, and his fingers formed fists.

"Yer drunk, Coley," Rat managed to utter. "I never hit a drunk before. Nor a kid, neither."

"You're not but a year older," Coley growled. "And a runt at that. As for hittin' folks, I never knew you to hit anybody at all. Now git out o' my way! Gal like Becky here'll appreciate a chance at somethin' better'n what she's seen so far!"

Hanks made a grab for Becky, but Rat intercepted the move and flung the young cowboy back on his heels.

"Walk, Coley," Rat said with a menacing glare. "I've warned you now. I'd hate to wallop a drunk, but if you don't leave, I vow to do just that!"

"Coley?" Orville Hanks called as he made his way through a gathering crowd. "Coley, don't."

"He asked for it, Grandpa," Coley said, stripping off his shirt and starting for Rat.

"Please, boys, this is a friendly gathering," John Morris said, trying to intervene. Coley knocked the man aside and took a wild swing. Rat deftly avoided it, and another besides. Coley was just nineteen, but he had powerful shoulders and half a foot longer reach. His third swing found Rat's left shoulder, and the next landed squarely against his face.

Pain chased restraint from Rat's being. He was mad as a bobcat, and when Coley swung again, Rat ducked and drove two hard right hands into the cowboy's sweat-streaked belly. As Coley recoiled, Rat let fly a left that crunched the young cowboy's cheekbone. A hard right to the cowboys nose followed.

"Grandpa?" Coley muttered as his legs gave way. Young Hanks dropped to one knee, wobbled a moment, and then collapsed in a heap.

"I'm sorry, Mr. Hanks," Rat said, licking his torn knuckles. "Did my best to dodge it, but he wouldn't listen."

"Want us to finish it, Mr. Hanks?" a trio of rowdies asked.

"Don't think that'd be altogether wise," Sheriff Cathcart said, stepping into the center of things. "Saw most o' it myself, Orville. Grandson or no, you got to see the truth o' things. Coley started the trouble, pressed it, and got himself paid in full."

"I'd say so," the elder Hanks agreed. "But it seems to me young Hadley there ought to pay a bit, too."

"For holdin' his ground?" the sheriff howled. "Not what you taught his pa, I'll wager. Now I figure everybody's about wasted enough effort on Coley tonight. Load him up in a wagon and take him along home."

"And if we don't" a cowboy asked.

"I'll lock him up myself," the sheriff answered. "Clear enough, Orville?"

Orville Hanks nodded, then motioned for a pair of cowboys to tend Coley.

"What the sheriff said's right," Hanks said, turning to Rat. "I can't fault a man for standin' up for himself, especially not if he's a Hadley. There's no backdown in your blood, is there, son? But it's a fool's play to go after a man with friends, Rat. Or my grandson."

Rat nodded at the rancher, but his blazing eyes returned the warning in kind. After all, it wasn't the smartest thing to tangle with Rat Hadley these days.

As the crowd dispersed, hands reached out to pat Rat's back. Others offered words of encouragement or appreciation. Afterward Rat took Becky's hand and led the way toward the food tables.

"I'm sorry for all the fuss," he told her. "I didn't mean to spoil this time."

"You haven't," she objected. "And Coley Hanks has been askin' for a thrashin' all his life."

"Still, yer pa's told me a hundred times to duck trouble."

"It's not always possible, though, is it?" she asked.

"Guess not," he confessed.

Later, as he sat alone on the porch staring at the stars and listening to Coley's taunts echo through his head, Rat could scarcely control his anger.

"Don't let it eat at you," the sheriff advised when he stepped through the doorway and joined Rat.

"Shouldn't've lost my temper," Rat grumbled.

"Hard words were spoken."

"None I ain't heard before, Sheriff."

"Didn't look to me like the words riled you half so much as when he grabbed Becky's hand."

"Guess that's true, but the words hit close to home."

"You know, Rat, there are those expected you wouldn't hold your own with Coley Hanks. He's done more'n his share o' brawlin', and he's got size and weight on his side."

"He was drunk," Rat muttered. "Besides, I been scrappin' one way or another most all my life. Thought I was past that now, though."

"Well, Erastus, don't you think some things are worth fightin' for?"

Rat turned and gazed into the serious eyes of Lem Cathcart. They held an almost fatherly pride.

"You think I did right, don't you?" Rat asked.

"By my tallyin', son. But what's truly important is what you think yourself."

Rat nodded. He'd known that all along, though.

Chapter Seventeen

That next morning Rat wasn't so satisfied with the results of the fight. He awoke to find the left side of his face purple and one eye near shut. His shoulder throbbed, and his hands ached.

"Pa, you ought to see Rat," Busby called when they approached the wash basin before breakfast.

"Well, folks'll know what you've been about," the sheriff said, examining Rat's eye with concern. "Best make a stop by Doc's place. Didn't know Coley had that much punch."

"Neither'd I," Rat confessed. "Got a hard jaw, too," he added, frowning at his abused knuckles.

"If you ask me, the Lord's trying to tell you something about fistfighting at fiesta," Cora Cathcart asserted.

"Maybe so, Ma," Buzz said, grinning. "But I'd bet Coley's a good deal worse off. Ain't liable to go callin' Rat names again anytime soon."

When they visited the doctor's surgery later that morning, Rat discovered Busby's suspicions were true. Coley Hanks lay asleep on Dr. Jennings's treatment table. His face looked like it had gotten too close to an exploding powder keg, and the rest of him didn't look much better.

"Guess I oughtn't to charge you, Rat," the doctor said as he painted a cut on Rat's forehead with iodine. "You bring me such good business and all."

"I believe I'm retirin' from that trade," Rat said, wincing from the sting of the medicine.

"Live longer that way, I'd judge. Still, I don't know what a doctor'd do without a bit of excitement now and again. You birth a few babies and treat little ones, but for challenges, give me a good brawl or a knife skirmish every time."

The doctor laughed, but Rat found nothing amusing about those remarks. He'd seen a man opened up by a knife in Kansas. Wasn't anything a doctor could do for that poor cowboy.

"You know, Rat, there's been a lot o' talk about you in town this mornin'," Doc Jennings said when he finished painting Rat's knuckles.

"Yeah?" Rat asked. "What're they sayin'?"

"This and that, but mostly they think maybe you'd make a good permanent deputy after Henning leaves."

"Sheriff already spoke to me 'bout that," Rat explained.

"Sheriff Cathcart's had a soft spot for you since fetchin' you to Thayerville from that villain Otto Plank. The Morrises speak for you when the talk comes your way. But before, people weren't any too certain you had the backbone to stand up for 'em. You went and settled that last night. Bet you find 'em a deal friendlier here on out."

"Figure a fistfight makes me a better sort, Doc?"

"No, Rat, it's not that at all. They saw Becky bothered, and they watched you take up for her. It's a good instinct, takin' up for the helpless."

"I wouldn't number Becky among the more helpless folks I run across in my time walkin' this earth."

"Well, that may be true. Still, there's the way you rode herd on the youngsters, too. Almost lost my teeth laughin' at the way you threw those Plank kids in the trough! You got a core in you, Rat, that's better'n most. Warms people to see it."

"I'd rather it mended my face," Rat grumbled.

"Time'll be doin' that," the doctor explained. "Now get along with you. I done what I can."

He returned to the Cathcart place, hoping to give his weary bones a rest. Instead he found Becky waiting for him.

"I see you got yourself looked after proper for once," she observed.

"Doc didn't even charge," Rat said, sitting beside her on the porch. "Said I was sendin' him business."

"I'm sorry you were hurt, Rat," she told him. "I don't think I thanked you proper last night, either."

"Thanked? For what, ruinin' yer night?"

"It wasn't ruined," Becky objected. "You may not realize it, but in defending my honor, you've made me into somewhat of a notable personage hereabouts. Why, I can't walk down the street without noticin' folks whisperin' and pointin'."

"I expect you could do without that."

"Rat, I've lived all my life in Thayerville, and this is the first time anyone besides an occasional stray dog or alley cat took notice o' me. I do feel sorry for declinin' Coley's dance, though."

"You do?"

"Your face paid a high price for my refusal."

"I been beat on before," Rat assured her. "I mend quick enough."

"I confess I enjoyed it some. Not just Coley gettin' his due. It isn't every girl has men fightin' battles for her hand, you know. Gives a body the notion maybe you care."

"You've known that awhile," he replied. "Truth is, I took to you the first time we swiped apple fritters off yer ma's table. You weren't but what, thirteen?"

"And you fifteen and half an inch shorter. I didn't think you'd recall that."

"Isn't much good I forget. And them fritters was tasty!"

"Oh, Rat," she howled. "Is that what you remember of it?"

"I recall you wore pigtails then. And you had the prettiest blue eyes in Texas. Then and now. I can tell even with one eye."

"And even with half a face turned blue, you're the man I'd share my future with."

"Becky?"

"Don't you think it's about time we get about the business o' gettin' married? I mean you been livin' here in my house goin' on half a year. We've shared about every color o' sunset there is. I've heard all about your dreams. Spring's come. It's time to plant."

"I'd never make much of a farmer," Rat muttered.

"Farmer?" she cried. "Who's talkin' nonsense? Have you forgotten all about that ranch you described?"

"It might not make a livin', Becky."

"Well, you could still work for Pa. Henning Lewis is off soon, and you know Pa expects you to take his place. We'd have enough to live on. You could use the reward money to buy a house and some land. That way you'd have a chance to add the horses a few at a time."

"It costs considerable to buy even a small place, though," Rat pointed out.

"Not more than five-hundred dollars."

"Ain't got five hundred," he said, frowning. "Only half that. Two-hundred fifty."

"What? I swore Pa said the reward was five hundred."

"It was," Rat said nervously.

"Then what became of the other two-hundred and fifty dollars?"

"I give it to Mitch Morris."

"For safekeepin'? Oh, Rat," she said shaking her head in disappointment. "He's a notorious gambler, you know. He surely threw it all away playin' cards.

"No, it was for payin' his debts," Rat explained. "Had a pair o' fellows after him. The money squared him."

"At the cost of our . . . your dream."

"Ranch can wait," Rat declared. "Mitch couldn't."

"I don't know what to say, Rat Hadley," Becky said, rising to her feet and pacing along the porch rail. "Sometimes I don't even know you. To throw away half a year's wages . . ."

"Weren't half a year's wages," he argued. "It's money come o' shootin' Curly Bob Clark. Wasn't earned by choppin' wood or roundin' up cattle. Come to me out o' nowhere."

"And you gave it away."

"No, I paid a debt," he told her. "Not Mitch's, either. Mine."

"You were playin' cards?"

"No, Becky. I give Mitch his life. Why not? He give me mine."

"That's nonsense, Rat. Pure nonsense. Mitch Morris never in his life did a thing for anybody. He's driven his folks past worry, shamed 'em in the eyes o' friends and neighbors. You don't owe him a thing, Rat."

"Yes, I do," he argued. "You say you don't know me. Well, maybe nobody in this world save Mitch really does. Ain't let many people inside me."

"Would you let me in?"

"There's a world o' pain there, Becky. You might not like what you find."

"I love you, Rat Hadley. That means sharin' whatever there is, be it pain or joy."

"Then let's find ourselves some horses. There's a place you ought to see."

So it was that Rat Hadley took Becky Cathcart out to the Brazos. It was country she, too, found familiar. As they passed cowboys riding fence lines or chasing steers out of hollows, Rat recounted his own cowboying days.

"Here's where that fool mustang pony rubbed the britches off me," he explained. "Same horse that kilt Pa."

They passed by a band of children swimming in the river. Rat stared hard at them, half expecting to recognize Alex or little Marcus. The faces all resembled Coley Hanks too much for comfort, and Rat led the way south toward the line cabin that had once been home. Rat paid little attention to the house. Instead he visited J. C. Hadley's lonely grave. Then he swung around and headed for the old Plank place.

"Maybe we'd best avoid this," Becky suggested. "Pa told me a frightful tale about old man Plank. You know his own son finally killed him."

"Efrem," Rat mumbled. "Gone outlawin' now. I heard Peter was runnin' the farm, but I don't see the fields planted. Miz Morris took in the littler ones."

"Peter left just after Christmas to try his luck in California," Becky explained. "I thought you knew."

"No. Guess I'm not the only one to see ghosts here."

"Tell me about it."

He frowned heavily as he stared at the old barn. It seemed as if Otto Plank stood there scowling, swinging a leather strap, and yelling Rat's name. Painful memories flooded his mind. And as he shared the nightmare tale, Becky alternately covered her eyes and gasped.

"I knew it was bad," she commented when he finished. "But how can a man beat his own children over such trifles? What manner o' devil locks boys in a barn?"

130

"Otto Plank did, Becky. And I guess in the end he paid for it. Me, I was lucky. I got away with only a few scars on my back."

"And others underneath?"

"Yeah, there's that," he confessed.

"I still don't understand how you could throw away two-hundred fifty dollars on Mitch Morris, though."

"You don't?" he asked. "Becky, you know why I'm not buried up here someplace?"

"I certainly do. It's because my pa rode up here and got you away from Otto Plank."

"The sheriff didn't come by himself, Becky. And he didn't come the first time at all. It was Mitch rode here, risked his hide to see I was well. Was his folks promised Ma to check, but they'd come on Sundays and leave when old man Plank got riled. Was Mitch who spied on me, come back with yer pa."

"You did things for him, too," she argued. "I recall him tellin' how you shot up a band of rustlers on the Cimarron River, saved the both of you. And there were times chasin' ponies . . ."

"Those were shared dangers, Becky," Rat said somberly. "They only tightened the bond. But I was here alone, with the Planks. Sure, yer pa took me into town, but it was the Morrises come and offered to take me in. It was his folks spoke, Becky, but a blind man could tell the offer was Mitch's. I owe him my life."

"You worked for your keep, didn't you?"

"Never as you'd know it. Truth is Mitch and I were often up to nonsense. Half a dozen times Miz Morris'd sent me on my way but for Mitch. And who else'd give a boy leave to run cows half the spring and take him back when Orville Hanks had no more use o' him? They sent me to school, and if I squawked 'bout my lessons, Miz Morris or Mitch'd sit me down and help me through 'em. Elsewise I'd never learned to read."

"It seems to me any debts incurred were long since satisfied," Becky said, gazing scornfully at Rat's tormented features.

"Not before," he answered. "Now, well, I bought Mitch his hide, so I guess we're even."

"And the ranch?"

"There's time for that," he assured her. "I make a good wage ridin' guard for the stage, and if you add what yer pa's promised for deputyin' on my off days, I'll have a fair sum saved again in no time."

"And when Mitch comes next time and needs another stake?"

"He won't," Rat declared.

"Won't he? I've watched how it is with gamblers, Rat. When their luck turns sour, they rarely stop playin'."

"What do you want me to do, promise I won't offer him money?"

"Yes, Rat, that's exactly what I want," she told him. "If we're to have a future, you can't drag leg irons around. That's what Mitch Morris has become, you know. To his family first. And now to you."

Rat frowned heavily. How was it Becky couldn't understand? Hadn't he explained what he and Mitch had shared? Didn't she know what it was like with brothers?

They returned to town shortly before dusk. Rat hadn't spoken a dozen words on the way back, and Becky had given up trying to stir up a conversation. She could read the pain on his face, and she said as much. "All that was long ago," she grumbled. "It's time to move on."

Rat left his horse at the Western's corral, then escorted Becky down Main Street to the livery. Halfway there a voice called out from the Lucky Lady. Mitch Morris stepped through the swinging doors, grinning broadly and waving a handful of fresh bank notes at his old friend.

"Rat, don't," Becky pleaded. But Rat returned Mitch's greeting nevertheless.

"Let go the bridle," Becky then demanded. She turned the horse and galloped away.

"Been ridin', I see," Mitch observed as he stepped over beside Rat.

"Was out to the river," Rat explained. "Past the Plank place."

"Didn't figure that'd be a place to bring you smiles."

"I took Becky. She wanted to know why I gave you the money."

"Oh," Mitch said, frowning. "Then I guess I'm to blame for her frown. Sorry, Rat."

"Not yer doin'."

"Sure, it is. I come to you for the money to pay my debts. Don't you worry, though, Rat. I got the cards goin' my way again. I swear to you. I'll pay back that money—and soon, too. Take that for a promise."

"Doesn't need repayin'," Rat grumbled.

"Sure, it does," Mitch argued. "Don't you think I see it in your eyes? I do believe I could live with anybody else in this world save you thinkin' ill o' me, Rat."

"I couldn't do it for long, Mitch. Too many recollections."

"I'm glad to hear that. It weighs on me how you looked when you give me that money. I'll earn it back real fast. Just you wait and see. Just you wait and see, Rat."

Rat tried to erase the doubt from his face. He wasn't entirely successful.

Chapter Eighteen

It seemed to Rat Hadley that trouble had a way of coming in full flood sometimes. His eye was still swollen from the fight with Coley Hanks, and Becky was in an ill humor to boot. He should have expected problems on the run to Albany and back.

The westbound leg went without a hitch. Of course Henning Lewis was aboard, finally off west for better pickings. Two of the company's other guards were passengers, too. Colonel Wyler had sent them up to help expand the company's Albany operations, what with the railroad spur near finished and cattle shipping certain to begin.

"Makes you feel downright comfortable," Pop Palmer declared as he nudged the horses along the trail. "Like to see them Oxenberg boys hit us today! Be a fine surprise for 'em, all right."

"I expect those fellows's off somewhere gold's easier to come by," Rat muttered. "If they depended on the Western for their livin', they'd be starved, the whole bunch o' them."

"Oh, they ain't so particular, Rat. Robbed a bank down at Weatherford last week. Blew one whole wall o' the place to kingdom come."

"I thought they were road agents."

"A thief'll be found round money. Them Oxenbergs ain't particular. Rob farms even. Kilt an old woman up on the Trinity back in February."

"You keep mighty close tabs on 'em," Rat observed.

"They been after me once, Rat. I take that personal. Best know the enemy, 'specially if it's a bunch likes to shoot folks."

Rat nodded. And when the coach finally pulled into Albany, he made a point of dropping by the town marshal's office to have a look through any posters that might warn of trouble.

"Anybody in particular you interested in?" the marshal asked after passing Rat a stack of wanted posters.

"Yessir," Rat admitted. "The Oxenberg gang."

"They'd be on the wall yonder," the lawman explained. "Trouble there is those boys take in new hands all the time. It's hard to catch 'em 'cause they know the country. And if they send out scouts, it's always the newest faces—ones we don't know."

Rat nodded. He gazed at the vague descriptions. The only faces sketched were the two Oxenbergs and a cold-eyed Efrem Plank. A fourth face was covered by a large X. The marshal had scrawled "shot in Jacksboro, March" alongside.

"Ain't far from here to Jacksboro," Rat observed.

"Got themselves spotted not half a week ago right here in Albany," the marshal grumbled. "But by the time I got some men to head 'em off, they'd up and vanished. You spot any signs comin' up from Thayerville?"

"Not a one," Rat answered.

" 'Course, they's clever. Wouldn't be leavin' tracks so just any fool could spot 'em."

"No, they'd keep to the shadows," Rat agreed. "Shame we cain't do the same. A stagecoach needs a wide trail."

That night Rat joined a half dozen Western employees in the saloon for a farewell drink with Henning Lewis.

"Joinin' the Rangers and marryin' yerself off in the same week," Rat said, laughing. "That's a man with an appetite for hard times sure."

"Me?" Lewis asked. "I ain't the fellow's got one side o' his face purple from fightin' that Hanks kid over Becky Cathcart!"

The others turned their laughter on Rat, and all he could do was grin and laugh along with them.

Rat didn't plan on staying more than a minute. The stage left early next morning on the easterly leg of the trip, and he was tired. Pop Palmer blocked his escape, though.

"Guess we ought to drink a farewell to Rat here, too," the driver declared. "He's sure to land Hen's old job, and I'll have another guard to break in."

"Well, now, that's news," the others cried, slapping Rat's back. "You sure know how to finish up a job, though."

"How's that?" Rat inquired.

"Don't you know?" Pop asked. "We got a special pay box to haul back. Thousands o' dollars in it."

"What?" Rat cried, gazing warily around the crowded saloon.

"Money pledged to the railroad," Lewis explained. "They had a bit o' trouble with outlaws o' late, so they switched it over to us so's to fool people."

"I expect that'd work better if you didn't go tellin' everybody in Albany o' it," Rat complained.

"Word's pretty much out already," Pop replied. "How do you figure we knew? The colonel sure ain't spreadin' the word."

"Somebody's sure done it," Rat muttered. "Best I get myself to bed early, Pop. Tomorrow's run seems like an invitation for trouble."

"That's why I got you along with me," the driver boasted. "Best shot around, and steady, too."

Palmer began to pour Rat another shot of whiskey, but the young guard declined. He was still grumbling to himself when he reached the Western stable where he planned to pass a peaceful night.

It didn't work out that way. Lurking gunmen haunted his dreams. He awoke to find himself fumbling around, searching for his rifle.

"Sorry I bothered you, Rat," a stableboy called. "Thought to open the shutters and let in some air."

Another time two stock handlers came in from a night of drinking and card playing. Finally Rat abandoned the loft and set off for the outskirts of Albany. He stretched out beneath a scrub mesquite and finally found some rest.

He returned to the stage office at dawn. After gobbling a hurried breakfast, he grabbed his rifle and stood watch while a pair of railroad men hauled the heavy chest atop the coach.

"Looks heavy," a familiar voice observed from the street. "Not carryin' the U. S. Mint, are you, Rat?"

Rat turned to gaze at Mitch Morris's easy smile.

"Lord, what's brought you so far west, Mitch?" Rat asked.

"Heard there was a game to be had hereabouts. Just about have enough to pay you back, old friend. Tomorrow should see it done. Hang around and I'll settle up."

"Be back in Thayerville tomorrow," Rat explained.

"On the coach?" Mitch asked. "Ma told me Deputy Lewis was leavin' and you'd been hired to take his place. Thought you'd be finished with all this other foolishness."

"It's a fair livin'," Rat argued. "Anyhow, the deputy's job ain't official exactly."

"I see," he said, frowning. "Well, you watch out, eh? I passed a pair o' suspicious characters comin' into town. Hard times bring out the worst in men, you know."

"Or the best," Rat argued. "Tests a man, I'll admit."

Mitch nodded, then turned to leave.

"Mitch, I got half an hour 'fore we pull out," Rat called. "Care to nibble a biscuit and talk?"

"I would," Mitch replied. "But I promised a fellow a game over at the hotel. He's got money just waitin' for my pockets, Rat. And later on yours."

"Well, good luck to you."

"Good luck yourself, Rat Hadley!"

Rat read rare concern in Mitch's eyes. Or maybe it was just reluctance—envy, even. To hear others talk, Mitch's luck was as elusive as ever. The cards hadn't brought much favor. But then things could change. Rat hoped the fellow at the hotel was not averse to losing.

Soon enough Rat set aside his concerns for Mitch. He busied himself loading trunks and cases atop the coach. He then assisted the passengers a moment. There were six of them in all. George Haslett, a well-known gambler, had worn out his Albany welcome, and a young cowboy named Bob Grant was off to Thayerville so Doc Jennings could have a look at a festering toe. Boyd Lambert and his wife Louise brought their two little girls in last. Pop Palmer then climbed atop the coach, and Rat followed.

Moments later the eastbound was bouncing along toward Thayerville.

Almost from the first Rat felt eyes on his back. After a bit he detected two trailing riders.

"Maybe we ought to turn back," Rat suggested.

"Ain't likely to set ill on the colonel's stomach if we do," Pop mumbled.

"I suppose they can hit us just as easy goin' that way as any other," Rat grumbled.

" 'Fraid so," Pop said as he hurried the horses along. Five miles later two more riders joined the pursuit. One took station on the left flank, and the other chose the right.

"I've had friendlier company," Rat observed, pointing to the flour sack masks the outlaws wore.

"Me, too," Pop declared. "Won't be long now, you know. We're closin' on the hills."

"Cain't help that," Rat replied, "but I can whittle on the odds some." He climbed back amid the valises and boxes, then made himself a makeshift parapet. The Winchester swung over at the left-hand rider, then exploded. Its bullet sped across the rocky landscape and slammed into the rider's chest. He toppled from his pony, and the other raiders instantly increased the range.

"That's one," Pop pointed out. "They got others, though."

Rat followed the driver's pointing finger toward the low hill just ahead. Five horsemen blocked the trail. Pop steered the horses toward a small pond. He then halted the coach and urged the passengers to seek cover.

"Give 'em the coach," Haslett advised. "It's all they want."

"Well, they won't get it," Rat vowed. "Not so long as I'm up here."

"Don't be crazy!" Pop cried. "There's too many."

"Maybe gettin' shot'll discourage 'em some."

Rat watched as the raiders formed a loose circle. They dismounted and began closing in immediately. A tall, thin bandit climbed atop a boulder, and Rat put a bullet through his shoulder. Another raced through a nearby ravine, firing wildly. Rat waited a second before putting a ball through his forehead.

"That's three o' you!" Rat yelled. "Anybody else want some?"

His answer wasn't long in coming. A volley of rifle fire tore through the coach and the surrounding rocks. The little Lambert girls took to wailing, and their mother pleaded for Rat to stop.

"No, you leave him to his work," Grant argued. "You wouldn't enjoy them outlaws' company a bit, Miz Lambert. They'd kill you, or maybe do worse."

"Hush," Lambert shouted. "I won't have you frighten my family."

"Then grab yerself a gun and help," Rat growled.

Bob Grant was doing that already. He wasn't any older than Rat, but he put a Colt pistol to good use. He killed one attacker and drove three others to cover.

"You got some spare shells?" Grant called.

"Right here," Rat called, grabbing a box from behind the driver's bench. As he tossed the ammunition to Grant, the cowboy exposed himself for a fraction of a second. That was long enough for a concealed rifleman to put a bullet in Grant's hip.

"Lord, I'm hit!" the cowboy screamed.

"Won't somebody help him?" Mrs. Lambert shrieked.

Haslett tried, but the raiders were closing in, and three shots traced the gambler's footsteps. A fourth shattered an elbow, and a fifth struck Haslett in the small of the back, toppling him into the pond.

"Let's go, boys!" the leader of the outlaws urged. Men hurried closer, and Rat opened up again. This time he had no success. Bullets now riddled the coach from close range, and Rat rolled off the side and tried to escape. A bullet shattered the Winchester's stock then, showering Rat's wrists with splinters. He howled in pain and discarded the useless rifle.

"It's over!" Pop Palmer yelled, waving a white kerchief. "We had enough!"

Five gunmen descended on the stage that moment, and the masked raiders quickly disarmed Pop Palmer and young Bob Grant. They busied themselves but a moment with the others, then herded the captives into a huddle.

"Well, we done just fine after all," their leader declared. "Ef, you and young Jim there fetch that box. Throw down the rest o' the things, too. Might be somethin' useful."

"Sure, Bo," the younger of the two agreed.

"You fellows keep usin' names, we might's well be done with these flour sacks," a tall, well-built man grumbled.

"Shoot, they know who we are," the leader argued, tearing off his mask. "Don't you sonny?"

The leader kicked Rat in his sore ribs, bringing a howl of pain.

"Yer posters don't do you justice," Rat told the face he recognized as

Bo Oxenberg. The bigger man would be his brother Oren. Rat recognized the empty gaze of Efrem Plank, too.

"Well, we couldn't give the artist much o' our time," Oren explained, spitting tobacco juice at Bob Grant's feet. "Ain't faces matter much anyhow. It's reputation. That brings men respect."

"Does it?" Rat asked as he painfully pried a long spinter from his hand.

"Take yours, Hadley," Oren added. "Word is you can shoot a flea off a dog's rump at a hundred yards. I didn't think it likely, but the way you shot Hi Hedges off his horse, I'm not so sure."

"Hi rode with us a long time," Bo added. "I don't like men to shoot my friends."

Bo swung his rifle over at Rat, then turned and fired instead at Bob Grant's hand. The cowboy rolled away clutching his bleeding fingers and wincing from the pain his hip wound brought.

"Don't be reachin' for yon pistol, boy!" Bo warned. "I'll fill you fuller o' lead than that gambler there."

"Do what you want to him," Ef Plank said, tossing the heavy chest onto the ground. "Rat there's an old friend o' mine, though. Cain't just up and shoot him, Bo. 'Sides, he's close to hitchin' himself to Lem Cathcart's gal over in Thayerville. I don't fancy havin' that ole hound on my trail."

"Nor me," Oren growled.

Rat gazed at Ef and managed a grateful nod. Ef went on with his work, though. Soon the outlaws were occupied wrenching open the money chest and tearing their way through trunks of clothes.

"Want to take the mail sack?" Ef asked as he held it up.

"You'll have the army after you," Pop warned.

"The army?" Oren asked. "They couldn't find dung in a stable. Take it along, Ef. I like to read the letters."

When the young outlaw called Jim broke open Louise Lambert's bag and began tossing the undergarments about, Boyd Lambert finally reddened.

"Stop that!" he yelled.

"That little lady must be a sight in these things!" Jim answered, tossing a stocking high in the air.

Lambert reached for something in his boot, but a pistol shot tore the hidden pistol from his hand.

"Mister, best not press your luck," a heretofore silent outlaw warned.

"I know you," Pop Palmer said, turning toward the masked raider.

"Lord Almighty! Mitchell Morris, you come of a good family. What brings you to rob my stage?"

"You old fool!" the gunman answered.

"Mitch?" Rat cried, staring in disbelief as features appeared familiar. There was something new and foreign as well—the glow of hatred. Rat sat transfixed, stunned, as Mitch raised his pistol and fired a solitary bullet into Palmer's large chest. The driver fell backward, and the gunman fired again.

"Mitch?" Rat called a second time.

"Who?" the shooter asked, turning the pistol on Rat.

"Fool boy," Oren Oxenberg yelled, rushing over and turning the masked killer away from the captives. "You done it now! Be hangin' sure to come o' this!"

"Mitch?" Rat shouted even louder. The masked figure never even turned, though. The Oxenbergs collected the cash from the money chest, loaded it in a pair of stockings, and tied the booty atop Bo's horse. Then the raiders remounted their animals and set off southward. Rat counted six, though one barely hung onto his saddle horn.

"They've gone," Mrs. Lambert announced. "Praise God. Let's get our things collected and be off."

"Things?" Rat screamed, bending over Pop Palmer. "We got people to see after."

"I'll have a look at the boy," Mrs. Lambert agreed. "The gambler's dead."

"I ain't!" Pop shouted. "Not yet, leastwise."

"We'll get you to town, Pop. I promise."

"I'll be elsewhere long 'fore you get this coach to Thayerville," Pop said, coughing violently. "You promise me somethin' else, Rat Hadley."

"Anything," Rat vowed.

"You promise to hunt down Mitch Morris and see him hung! He's kilt me, Rat. See he pays for that!"

"Pop, don't ask that o' me," Rat implored. "I'll help with yer little ones. I'll be like a big brother to 'em all."

"I know that," Pop grumbled. "Shoot, nobody ever needed speak on it. I got friends aplenty, Rat, to help 'em. What I need's a man to track a killer!"

"You cain't even be sure it was Mitch," Rat argued. "I know him. He couldn't . . ."

"I know him, too," Pop said, fixing a vice-like grip on Rat's tortured hands. "Promise me!"

"I'll see it done," Rat said, trembling. "And yer family looked after, too."

"Bless you, son. Never figured it'd be young Mitchell. Shoot, I took him ridin' when he wasn't yet Wade's size. That was back in . . ."

Pop Palmer never finished. He coughed, and then his eyes rolled back. Death had claimed him.

Chapter Nineteen

The eastbound stage pulled into Thayerville three hours late. Sheriff Lem Cathcart was pacing in front of the stage office alongside Nate Parrott when Rat managed to rein in the horses and halt the coach. It wasn't easily done. Even though Louise Lambert had pulled the worst of the splinters from his hands, she'd done nothing to stop the aching.

"They've had trouble," Parrott announced. "Told you."

"Rat?" the sheriff called. "Where's Pop?"

"Inside," Rat said as he pulled the brake. "He's dead, Sheriff. There's a gambler in there kilt, too, and a cowboy bad hurt."

The sheriff nodded, then opened the door and helped the Lamberts climb out. Their ashen faces testified to the trials of the journey. Nate Parrott hollered for a pair of freight handlers and dispatched a boy for Dr. Jennings.

"Who was it?" the sheriff demanded to know. "How'd it happen?"

"Ambush," Rat answered as he climbed down from the stage. "They hit us in the hills."

"Who?" Cathcart asked.

"The Oxenbergs," Rat said, "Seemed to be them anyhow."

"Lord, Sheriff, look at his hands," Parrott cried. "They look to've swollen double."

"Splinters," Rat explained. "My rifle shattered. If I'd just been able to hold 'em off . . ."

"No one man's goin' to fight them Oxenbergs," the sheriff said. "Come on, son. Let's hurry you down to Doc's and see 'bout them hands."

"He's got the cowboy to tend."

"That won't take forever, you know," Cathcart pointed out. "After your hand's tended, I want you to have a look at some posters."

"Yessir," Rat agreed.

The sheriff escorted Rat to Dr. Jennings's surgery. As for the doctor, he was heading up the street to the stage office to have a look at Bob Grant.

"Best sit yourself down, son, and wait on the doc," Cathcart suggested.

"Won't be much to it, Sheriff," Rat said, turning his hands over. "Just need some drainin'. When're we goin' after 'em?"

"Lord, Rat, ain't you had enough o' them? They're sure to be halfway to the next county by now."

"Not all of 'em," Rat declared. "One's hit bad. And their horses been rode hard."

"They shouldn't have so much trouble findin' horses."

"We goin' or not?"

"I'll spread the word we need men. Won't be hard puttin' a posse together. People thought a lot o' Pop."

"Yessir, they did," Rat agreed.

Sitting alone in the doctor's small office, Rat closed his eyes and tried to forget the nightmare raid. It wasn't possible. He kept seeing Pop Palmer, heard over and over again his cry for vengeance.

Doc Jennings returned to his surgery half an hour later. He looked haggard, and his trousers were spattered with blood.

"How's Grant?" Rat asked.

"Poor," the doctor grumbled. "Won't walk anytime soon, and he's lost a couple o' fingers. All in all he's lucky by my reckoning, though. There's two stretched out dead down there. Sheriff said you caught some splinters in your hands."

Rat raised his swollen hands, and the doctor scowled. He set his bag down on a small table, filled a basin with alcohol, and scrubbed.

"Come on over here, Rat," Doc Jennings instructed, pointing to a long table. "Got some diggin' ahead o' me."

Rat lay on the table, wincing as the doctor dug fragments of wood from each hand in turn. The pain was a torment, but he almost welcomed it for the distraction it provided. He knew pain, after all. He understood it. It was madness left him confused, and there had been too much of that lately.

"There's the last one out," Dr. Jennings finally announced as he set his needle aside and grabbed a bottle of iodine. "Seems like lately you been keepin' me busy," he added as he dabbed the reddish-orange liquid over Rat's hands. I'd advise givin' trouble a wide berth for a day or two. These fool hands'll stay swollen awhile, you know. Soak 'em in cool water. That'll help."

"No cool water where I'll be headed," Rat said as he rolled off the table and examined the doctor's handiwork. "I promised Pop I'd see his killers caught."

"We got a sheriff for that."

"I know. He's asked me to be his deputy."

The doctor started to argue, but Rat dug two silver dollars out of his pocket, tossed them onto the treatment table, and headed back to the stage office. Halfway there he was intercepted by Ned Wyler.

"Colonel?" Rat gasped. "Didn't expect you here."

"I came in to handle the transfer of the money chest," Wyler explained. "We had some trouble, I understand."

"They got it, Colonel. Shot Pop Palmer, too."

"What's your view on the raiders, Hadley? Sheriff Cathcart says it might be the Oxenberg brothers."

"Looked like 'em. I shot a couple of 'em. Then a bullet shattered my rifle, and . . ."

"I heard all that from the others."

"They shouldn't be too hard to track," Rat declared. "I know every inch o' that Brazos country."

"I don't know if that's much of an edge," Sheriff Cathcart said, joining the conversation. "Miz Lambert says Pop recognized one of 'em. Local boy, she says. Just who was it, Rat?"

"Efrem Plank," Rat said nervously. "He spoke up for me, Sheriff, and most likely saved my life."

"We knew about Ef," Cathcart muttered. "You sure there wasn't somebody else?"

"I've got my notions," Rat confessed. "If I'm right, we'll find him up on the river. If I'm wrong, better his family not suffer for my mistake."

"I, uh, see your point," the sheriff said, eyeing Wyler. "You fit to ride, son?"

"Eager," Rat answered.

"Best see Cora 'bout packin' us up some food," Cathcart advised. "I'm meetin' the rest at the livery in half an hour."

"I'll send some men," Wyler declared.

"Rather you kept 'em here unless they're local," the sheriff replied. "Hard country out by the river. Best I know my company."

"I understand," Wyler said, nodding. "Nate can choose a pair for you familiar with the land. You trust his judgment?"

"He's a good man. Rat, you get along to the house now. Not much time to waste."

"Yessir," Rat answered, hurrying on his way. He glanced back as he crossed the street and was surprised to find the sheriff still conversing with Colonel Wyler. The colonel was bound to have his questions, Rat supposed, what with the robbery and two men dead.

Rat found Becky waiting when he reached the house. Busby and Mrs. Cathcart were there as well.

"The sheriff said I should get you to pack some food, ma'am," Rat told Mrs. Cathcart.

"Is he takin' out a posse?" Buzz asked.

"Yeah, we leave in half an hour," Rat explained.

"Wish I could go," the boy grumbled. "Guess I'm too young."

"Be glad," Rat said, dropping to one knee so he could stare intently into Busby's eyes. "Ain't nothin' but death waitin' out there, Buzz. No adventure. Just killin' and dyin'."

"Your hands!" Becky shouted.

"Got some splinters," he explained as he hurried to collect some clothes and a blanket from the side room. He did so, then returned to the kitchen.

"Can't you stop long enough to tell us what happened?" Becky said, gripping his arm. "All we heard was that the stage was held up."

"I don't know much more'n that myself," Rat told her. "There will be time to talk later."

"Will there?" Becky asked. Concern painted her face.

"Sure," he said, sighing. Mrs. Cathcart handed over a flour sack full of supplies, and he slung it over one shoulder, rammed his blanket roll under the opposite arm, and set off for the livery.

Men were assembling there already. Others came, too, for the stableman, Bart Medway, was also the best carpenter in town. He was already at work on two coffins. Meanwhile Pop Palmer and the gambler rested in a wagon bed.

Rat left the provision sack and his blanket roll with Nate Parrott before racing to the corral to fetch his mustang. The animal was already saddled, and Rat merely checked the cinch. Once satisfied, he led the animal back to the livery. That was when he saw Varina Palmer and Pop's children. Almost immediately Tyler raced over and leaned against Rat's side.

"Pa's dead," the boy whispered. "Shot all to pieces."

"I was there," Rat muttered.

"You were supposed to guard him," the boy said accusingly.

"Tried," Rat explained. "I wasn't good enough, or maybe there were just too many of 'em."

"That's what Sheriff Cathcart says. You'll find 'em, though, won't you?"

"I promised Pop," Rat said, guiding Tyler back to his family. "You don't break a promise made to a man like Pop."

"I promised him I'd take care o' things while he was gone," Tyler said as they walked.

"Be plenty o' men around to help," Rat observed. "You put me at the top o' the list, Ty."

The boy managed a brief grin before grief overwhelmed him.

Rat offered his respects to Mrs. Palmer, and for a few moments they shared a few of Pop's stories and remembered better times. Then Sheriff Cathcart announced it time to mount up, and Rat made his farewells.

"I know you feel bound to join 'em," Varina said, "but Pop thought highly o' you, Rat. Don't get yourself kilt."

"Don't plan to," he assured them. "You boys watch out for yer mother. Stay pretty, Velma. You were always Pop's pride."

"We know," Velma admitted.

Rat bent and kissed the girl's forehead before hurrying back to the posse. After handing Sheriff Cathcart the provisions, Rat tied the blanket roll behind his saddle and mounted his pony.

"Here, Rat, have a look at these," the sheriff said, passing over a handful of wanted posters. "See anybody familiar?"

"They spoke o' this Hedges fellow," Rat explained. "And even masked, I could tell Oren and Bo Oxenberg."

Rat gazed at the others, but he matched no faces.

"The other two I noticed were Ef and a young fellow named Jim," Rat said, passing the posters back to the sheriff.

"And the one that shot Pop?"

"We talked about him already, Sheriff. Cain't be sure."

The lawman nodded, then passed Rat a rifle.

"Be needin' it," Cathcart declared. He then formed the posse into a single file.

Sheriff Cathcart sent two of the riders home, deeming their horses unfit. He sifted through the rest, dismissing a man here and there. Finally he settled on an even dozen.

"Let's ride, boys," Cathcart called, and the men howled their agreement.

Sheriff Cathcart led the way west, but soon he motioned Rat ahead. The stage route kept to even terrain and was longer by several miles than the cross-country trails Rat chose. It was hard going in places, what with crumbling ravines to cross and creeks to splash through.

"You and Mitch Morris used to pass time out this way, didn't you, son?" the sheriff asked as he pulled even with Rat fifty yards ahead of the others.

"Yessir," Rat admitted.

"Haven't seem much o' Mitch the last few weeks. Mary got a letter from him posted in Albany, though. Didn't come across him up there, did you?"

Rat's eyes betrayed the truth, and the sheriff nodded grimly.

They rode the next hour without sharing a word. Then Rat led the way toward the battle-scarred pond. Even now odds and ends of clothing lay about, interspersed with brass casings and discarded letters. The money chest remained open, haunting the scene.

"There's a fellow dead over here," Powell Hobbs called, pointing to a masked corpse. Another was nearby.

"That's Rufe Berry," one of the freight handlers declared when the dead men were unmasked. "Used to work horses in Ft. Worth."

"Other one's young Henry Allison," Hobbs added. "Hard news for his family."

"No need they should know," Sheriff Cathcart announced. "Bury 'em here."

"I shot one back up the trail, too," Rat said, waving in that direction.

"Could be Hedges," Cathcart muttered. "Let's have a look. These fellows'll stay busy a moment."

The two of them set off up the trail a half mile. Rat spied a riderless horse grazing nearby. Riding over, he located the lifeless body a dozen yards away.

"Yup, it's him," the sheriff agreed after tearing away the mask. "Hundred dollars reward on him, Rat. That your bullet in him?"

"Yessir. Fired from my old Winchester."

"The reward's a fair return on a shattered rifle."

"But not much payment for Pop," Rat grumbled.

"Maybe the Oxenbergs will be," Cathcart said. "They're worth a thousand each, you know."

"Not for much longer," Rat vowed, turning his horse and swinging around in order to pick up the outlaws' trail.

Chapter Twenty

Once the slain outlaws were buried, Sheriff Cathcart got the posse mounted and riding in short order. The men were eager to catch their quarry.

"How many of 'em will we hang?" Powell Hobbs asked. "There's a dozen sets o' tracks by my count."

"No, just six," Rat argued.

"Can we hang 'em all, Sheriff? Or just the ones Rat saw shootin'?" Hobbs asked.

"They were masked," Nate Parrott pointed out. "Could be any of 'em. I say haul the bunch o' them in for hangin'."

"It's a long way to haul a man," Hobbs muttered. "And some o' them'll put up a fight."

"Any what survive go to trial," Cathcart explained. "You boys all understand that, I hope."

The men grinned and nodded.

"They'll get the same trial Pop got," someone declared, and the rest howled their agreement.

Rat moved out ahead of his companions, but he could still hear their boasts and taunts. Most of the talk dealt with the generous reward offered for the Oxenbergs. Two thousand dollars, after all, brought out the worst in men.

"Brought too many by half," the sheriff complained as he pulled alongside. "I'd feel better, too, if we had a couple more accustomed to firin' rifles than flappin' their jaws."

"Sure," Rat agreed. "We may favor numbers if it comes to a fight, though. It will, don't you think?"

"Would seem likely, knowin' outlaw habits."

Rat frowned and urged his mustang into a trot. The sooner it was over, the better he'd feel.

The country north to the Brazos was rocky and hostile. A man could lose a trail there easy, and more than once the tracks of horses seemed to up and disappear. Often Rat searched creek bottoms or tangled brush for signs. Twice the sheriff spread the posse in a fan in order to pick up the outlaws' trail.

"I see somethin' yonder," Kyle Best, one of Parrott's horse handlers, called toward dusk.

"Over there on the left, Sheriff," Jack Sharpe, the town barber, added.

Cathcart waved Rat along, and the two of them rode to investigate. They found a bloody body lying in a mass of briars.

"Recognize him?" the sheriff asked.

"It's probably the one I shot down at the pond," Rat answered. "I never saw his face before, though."

The posse located a second corpse a half mile past the first one.

"Toby Hatcher," Sharpe announced. "Rides the Circle H fence line."

"Likely come upon the Oxenbergs by accident," Sheriff Cathcart surmised. "Poor luck that boy had. Best bury him. We'll send word along to the ranch when we finish up."

The grisly sight of Hatcher's body darkened the eyes of the posse members. Rat noticed there were few boasts now. Instead a sort of grim determination drove them onward. But as darkness fell, they had yet to catch up with the fleeing bandits.

"We goin' to stop soon, Sheriff?" Best asked. "My horse's near done in, and I'm not much better."

"Figure 'em to've crossed the river, Rat?" Cathcart called.

"No," Rat said, pointing to a yellow glow on a low ridge two or three miles ahead. "That'd probably be them there."

"Let's bring this business to a close then," the sheriff suggested. "Lead away, son."

Rat departed the trail and slowly picked his way across the darkened landscape. It was slow, treacherous going now. The moon had yet to rise, and only the faintest outlines of mesquite trees and rocks emerged from the gray darkness. The ground was familiar, though, and Rat led his companions down a dry creek bed and along into the hills beyond. He could smell bacon frying in a skillet, and rough talk danced on the wind.

Rat knew it was the Oxenbergs. He felt it in his soul. Few words could be made out for certain, but "Bo" and "Oren" were among the ones that could. The posse fanned out, then dismounted. Even as Rat crept toward the bright yellow flames of the campfire, shots shattered the night air.

"Lord, I'm shot!" Jack Sharpe screamed. Rifles spit bullets at unseen enemies, and men raced about in madness. Sheriff Cathcart shouted orders, and the Oxenberg brothers did the same. For the most part, though, it boiled down to men groping around helplessly, firing blindly, and praying to survive.

"Knew we should've moved on!" Bo Oxenberg shouted. "Who's up there anyhow?"

"Lem Cathcart!" the sheriff answered. "Best give it up, boys!"

"Ain't us takin' bullets, Cathcart!" Oren yelled. "I figure you three men short already, and more's sure to die."

The sheriff didn't reply. Instead he inched closer to the fire, hoping to detect some shadow of a target. Rat moved over beside Cathcart and motioned to the left.

"I see him," Sheriff Cathcart noted. "One o' ours?"

"Not unless our people's wearin' flour sacks on their heads."

"Lead away, son."

Rat nodded, then clawed his way along the rocky side of a cliff. He quickly got above the cowering outlaw. The sheriff followed. Then, with a wave, he signaled Rat to open fire. Both men rapidly blazed away. The raider never had a prayer. He was simply blown apart.

The sudden fury of the attack quickened Rat's blood. It broke the spirits of the remaining outlaws, too. A pair of them tried to flee toward the river, but their escape was blocked by Nate Parrott and the stock handlers. One man stumbled and fell. The other was shot down instantly.

The Oxenbergs took full advantage of the chance to make their own escape. They raced toward their horses, threw themselves atop the bare-backed animals, and kicked them into a gallop. As they rode past the fire, Rat had his first good shot at the thieves. He aimed and fired in the same motion, but the horse turned, and the bullet meant for Bo Oxenberg's head struck his brother in the hip.

"Bo, let's clear out," Oren urged. Rat rammed the Winchester's lever down and up again, only to discover his magazine was empty. In dismay he watched the Oxenbergs escape into the night.

"Hang it all!" Rat cried, stomping his foot angrily.

A pistol bullet whined through the air, and Rat dropped to the ground.

"Hold yer fire there!" Rat shouted. "I'm no outlaw."

"I am," the voice of the fallen raider called. "That you, Rat?"

Rat recognized Ef Plank's voice. It had been years since they shared the horrors of Otto's barn, but Rat could hardly forget Ef's urging the Oxenbergs toward mercy that very afternoon.

"You hurt, Ef?" Rat asked.

"Shot proper," the former farm boy explained. "Not so much I can't kill somebody, though."

"Let me help," Rat offered. "We can get you to a doctor."

"Why bother?" Ef asked. "I'm bound to hang. You tell Peter I went game, won't you? And look in on Vesty and Randy if the chance happens by."

"Ef?"

Efrem Plank then managed to rise to his feet. Blood gushed from a wound in one thigh, and both ankles were shattered. There was blood seeping through his shirt as well. Even so, the young bandit raised both pistols and opened up on the shadows. Two rifles barked an answer, throwing Ef backward against a tree.

"Ef?" Rat called again as he raced forward. Even in the dim light Rat could see a wistful smile on Efrem Plank's face. His eyes were still. He'd found his peace.

"Collect the dead," Cathcart told Nate Parrott. "Rat, let's get along after the others."

"It's grown dark," Rat objected. "Won't it wait for mornin'?"

"Let's go," the sheriff beckoned, and Rat reluctantly followed. They located their horses and mounted up. No sooner had they set out than the others joined them.

"Didn't figure to keep the reward all to yourself, did you, Sheriff?" Kyle Best asked.

"Lord," Cathcart grumbled. "We'll sound like a brigade o' preachers comin' down on 'em."

"Best we wait for mornin'," Rat muttered.

"Guess so," the sheriff reluctantly agreed. "Nothin' else'd work."

So it was that the Thayerville posse returned to the Oxenbergs' camp. Nate Parrott and two others had dragged the dead outlaws over near the fire. Nearby Jack Sharpe moaned. Parrott was dressing the barber's wounded shoulder.

"Turned doctor, have you?" Rat called.

"Nobody else to do it," Parrott complained.

"Powell's hurt, too," young Best declared.

"Ain't nobody helpin' him," Sharpe said, pointing to a figure shrouded by a saddle blanket. "Hit right in the forehead. Never a chance for him."

The riders dismounted and gathered beside their slain comrade. Suddenly the blood lust vanished. Death had struck close, it seemed.

"Tend your horses," the sheriff instructed. "Then get somethin' to eat and go to sleep. We'll be at it early tomorrow."

"Ain't we done enough?" Sharpe asked. "These fellows got to be the Oxenbergs, don't they?"

"Oren took a bullet, but Bo's well enough," Rat told them. "They got away, but ain't likely to make much distance."

"There was another one escaped, too," Cathcart added. "Rode off west."

"Well, I ain't goin' anywhere but back to town," Sharpe vowed. "We got the money, after all."

"We did?" Cathcart asked.

"Was in these stockin's," Parrott explained, pausing a moment from his doctoring to lift the stuffed stockings. "Most of it anyhow. I'd guess a couple or three hundred's gone, but I don't figure the colonel's apt to quibble 'bout that. After all, we got the mail, and it's scarce been touched."

"Colonel Wyler might be generous, eh?" Best declared. "Offer up a reward."

"I'm sure of it," Parrott agreed.

"Then I'm finished," a burly farmer named Waller announced. "Ain't eager to get myself kilt like ole Hobbs there."

Others muttered like sentiments, and the sheriff sighed.

"Was too many o' us for this anyhow," he replied. "Come daybreak those that want can take Jack back to town. Carry poor Hobbs back, too."

"And the outlaws?" Rat asked.

"Leave 'em to rot," Best suggested.

Rat read his companions' sour feelings. They couldn't erase Ef's favor, though. Once the others were settled into their blankets, Rat took a discarded spade from the Oxenberg camp and dug Efrem Plank a shallow grave. It was the best possible in that rocky ground, and Rat covered it with rocks to fend off wolves.

Strange how things turn out, Rat thought as he turned to rejoin the others. *Here Ef's buried, and I'm goin' to find myself called a hero and paid a reward. Wasn't a thimble's difference in the two of us, and now he's dead.* But it wasn't really Ef Rat Hadley was thinking about. No, his mind was fixed on the masked outlaw who'd coldly gunned Pop Palmer.

Couldn't be, Rat argued. *Not Mitch.*

But his heart remained unconvinced.

Morning found Rat tossing in his blankets. When Sheriff Cathcart shook him awake, Rat found the camp already astir. Half the posse was bound for town. The sheriff, Nate Parrott, Kyle Best, and the Turley brothers were determined to go on.

"Cain't be any other way," Clem Turley explained. "Hoyt Palmer's my cousin." His brother Charlie nodded.

"Makes six with Rat," Parrott pointed out. "Two-to-one odds if it comes to a fight."

"It will," the sheriff assured them. "Ain't nothin' but a noose waitin' them Oxenbergs. I don't figure it to come easy."

Rat never knew anything to come easy that could be hard. Oren was shot, though, and that narrowed matters some. The killers would be close by.

"What do you think?" the sheriff asked as he passed Rat a cold biscuit. "Trail leads south."

"They won't go that way long," Rat said, frowning. "There's a creek out there. They'll use it to cover their tracks."

"You imagine 'em that clever even with a bullet in Oren?"

"They been out here a long time accordin' to the posters, Sheriff. You stop thinkin' in this country, yer buzzard bait pretty quick."

"So what do you suggest?"

"We do it like before. I'll scout ahead. You follow with the rest. Let 'em play their tricks. I got the scent."

Oren and Bo Oxenberg used every ounce of skill they knew to conceal their trail. They rode through the creek and into the Brazos. They released their horses and sent them galloping up a false trail. But Rat detected brown drops of dried blood leaked from Oren's wound and followed them to a nest of boulders overlooking a bend in the river.

"There you are," Rat whispered as he spied the brothers huddling beside a small fire. Their wet clothes dried on a nearby clothesline. Rat didn't envy them passing the chilly spring eve like that. For a moment he thought of fetching his Winchester from its scabbard and shooting the outlaws then and there. But though he held the raid and the shootings against them, he'd lost his taste for cold-blooded execution. Shooting even the Oxenbergs naked by their breakfast fire offended Rat Hadley's sense of fairness.

Rat crawled back to his horse, then mounted the animal and returned to the posse. Sheriff Cathcart greeted the news with a smile.

"Looks like this's it, boys!" he shouted to the others. "We got 'em cold."

"Let's be about it then," Parrott replied.

Sheriff Cathcart took charge of the capture attempt. Nobody was much fooled by the words used. There wasn't any capture to it. The posse was out for blood, and the Oxenbergs were certain to oblige. Nevertheless Lem Cathcart formed the men in a loose arc, then encircled the Oxenberg brothers. The sheriff dismounted, and the others followed suit. Then Cathcart crawled closer.

"Bo, Oren, we got you surrounded!" Cathcart yelled. "Give it up!"

"They's here!" Oren cried, shaking his brother to life.

The two near naked outlaws made a scramble for their clothes and collected their guns on the way. Bo pulled on trousers and fired wildly with a pistol. Oren forsook his clothes and concentrated on a rifle. Neither stood a chance. Sheriff Cathcart put his first shot through Oren's knee, and a whole volley caught Bo, spun him like a top, and sent him crawling toward cover. He might have made it if Rat Hadley hadn't been waiting.

"I knew we should've kilt you, mister!" Bo grumbled as he fought to lift his rifle.

"Yeah, you should've done it all right," Rat agreed as he pulled his own trigger. The bullet split the outlaw's skull and killed him instantly.

"Bo?" Oren shouted. Six rifles turned on the large man, and he was struck four times. Bleeding severely, Oren tried to crawl to his brother. Nate Parrott fired again, and Oren's head snapped back as he fell on his face, dead.

"It's really them this time!" Best shouted as he hurried toward the fallen outlaws. "Figure I can have Oren's Colt, Sheriff? It's pure famous, you know."

"Help yourself," Cathcart replied. "Nate, why don't you see if you can find the rest o' that money?"

"Oren's sure not hidin' any o' it," Clem said, turning the naked outlaw over.

"I'll have a look at Bo," Charlie promised.

In the end, though, the outlaws had little save a few coins and some food scraps. Sheriff Cathcart dragged them to the river and washed off the worst of the blood. Rat then helped dress the corpses. No reward would be paid without evidence, and the best kind was the body of the criminal.

"Just about finished now," Cathcart said as he helped tie the corpses atop a pair of horses brought along from the outlaw camp. "Just one left to catch now. Eh, Rat?"

"Yeah, just one," Rat agreed.

"Sheriff, why not let him be?" Parrott asked. "It's the Oxenbergs were back of it. Like as not this other one's some poor out-o'-work cowboy or a farm boy out to have some adventure."

"No, he could be the one shot Pop Palmer, eh, Rat?" the sheriff replied.

"Yeah," Rat confessed. "But we don't know what he looks like or anything."

"We know enough," Cathcart argued. "Nate, if you and young Kyle there care to drag the Oxenbergs back, go ahead. Tell Cora I'll be along soon. You Turleys'll be stayin', won't you?"

"Bound to," Clem replied.

"Rat, you got a choice to make," the sheriff said.

Rat knew what was meant. Turning away meant no deputy's badge, no respect. Going on offered . . .

For a moment Rat imagined himself splashing away in the river, trading taunts with Mitch or racing Alex. Was that world so far away now?

"Rat?" the sheriff called.

"I promised Pop," Rat reminded them. "Besides, I figure I know where he'll be."

Chapter Twenty-One

As Rat Hadley led Lem Cathcart and the Turley brothers along the river, he couldn't escape feeling lost. Here, where he knew every rock and twig like an old friend! It seemed everything was changing, though. Soon he'd be bringing the world down on the best friend he had ever known.

Yes, Rat told himself. When they reached the end of the outlaw's trail, they would find Mitch Morris.

"Can't let it eat at you, son," the sheriff whispered as he joined Rat ahead of the others. "It wasn't your doin'. A man breaks the law, he puts himself at odds with decent people. You never twisted Mitch's arm, turned him toward this trade."

Rat wasn't so certain. Why were there only three-hundred dollars missin' from the cash box's loot? Wouldn't that cover Mitch's debt and leave him fifty dollars for a stake?

"I'll pay you back," Mitch had said time and again. Was this his only way?

A dozen memories drifted in and out of Rat's head during the hour it took to reach the rocky hill where old Tom Boswell had been buried. Rat saw himself younger, haggard, without hope. And he recalled Mitch welcoming him into the little room they shared.

"Guess we're brothers of a sort," Mitch had said. "That's somethin' for always, ain't it?"

"Sure," Rat had said. But maybe it was only another of those fragile bonds too easily broken. He'd lost his father, his home, and his family. Nothing was ever for always.

"Best we ford here," Rat called loudly, pointing to a break in the high rock walls that now encased the river.

"No need to rouse the dead," Cathcart warned as he waved for the Turleys to follow. "Nor anybody else."

Rat frowned. Perhaps he'd been trying to do just that. There was another ford a half mile back. Going that way, a man could come up on the hill from behind. Rat would have come that way if the Oxenbergs had been there. But he thought Mitch deserved to be met face to face.

And what if he's lyin' in ambush? Rat asked himself. Another scene appeared in Rat's mind—a masked outlaw shooting Pop Palmer. Was it possible Mitch had changed so much?

The four remaining members of the posse slowly splashed into the shallows and made their way across to the far bank. The cool water tormented the mustang, but its chill touch brought Rat back to the present. For a few moments his mind cleared, and he looked only to the business at hand. Once out of the river, he headed straight for the familiar hillside. The giant white oak seemed almost to be brooding.

You know, don't you, tree? Rat spoke silently. Then he nudged his horse past the charred remains of old campfires and along to where a solitary figure sat whittling a piece of juniper bark.

"Howdy, Rat!" Mitch called. "Never figured you for a visit. Thought you'd be busy with the stage and all."

"That was yesterday," Rat reminded his old friend. "Next swing's back to Albany tomorrow."

"So what brings you to this ole place?"

"Come with Sheriff Cathcart," Rat said gravely. "We been chasin' the Oxenberg gang."

"Oxenbergs?" Mitch cried in alarm. "Here?"

"No, they had their camp a few miles east o' here."

"You found 'em then?"

"Kilt 'em. Only one fellow got away. We figure he had some o' the cash from the holdup with him."

"Holdup?"

"They hit the stage just south o' here yesterday. Shot a passenger. And Pop Palmer."

"Not Pop!" Mitch exclaimed. "He was one fine man. You ain't found the one who shot him yet?"

"Yeah, we found him," Lem Cathcart said, joining the two old friends. "Mitch, I think it best if you shed that pistol on your hip. And if you still carry a hideout Colt, toss it aside, too."

"I don't understand," Mitch complained.

"Yeah, you understand just fine, I figure," the sheriff said, dismounting and walking slowly up to Mitch. Cathcart cautiously drew the revolver from Mitch's holster, then pried a smaller pistol from a boot.

"What's all this about?" Mitch cried. "Rat?"

"We followed a trail from the outlaw camp," Rat explained. "It come to the river and disappeared, but it was headin' straight here. And anyhow, I knew you'd be here."

"How?"

" 'Cause it's always been our refuge, ain't it, Mitch? You got some bad trouble this time. Cain't money buy you out o' it."

"Just what do you think I did?" Mitch asked.

"You shot Pop Palmer," the sheriff accused. "Didn't you?"

"I surely did not!" Mitch growled. "Look, Sheriff, I know you held against me that gambler in Thayerville, but I been keepin' my nose clean since then."

"Mitch, you shot another fellow since then!" Rat yelled. "And now Pop. Cain't deny it. I was there!"

"You saw me? Ain't possible."

"How's that?" the sheriff asked.

"Nobody could've seen me kill anybody," Mitch swore.

" 'Cause you had a flour sack over your face?" Cathcart asked. "Pop recognized your voice. Can you imagine Rat wouldn't't?"

"You tole 'em it was me, Rat?" Mitch cried.

"You sayin' it wasn't, Mitch?" Rat answered. "Swear it wasn't you, and . . .

"You'll what?" the sheriff asked. "Believe him?"

"If he's the one kilt Hoyt, let's get a rope, Sheriff," Clem Turley urged. "If he ain't, let's get after the one did it."

"Well, Sheriff?" Mitch asked, staring hard at the lawman. "Even you ain't sure. Show me some proof."

"Proof's lyin' in a casket at the livery," Cathcart grumbled.

"Listen to me," Mitch pleaded. "You all of you know me. Shoot, my ma and pa give you Hurleys credit when your farm was near busted. I used to haul supplies to you when you couldn't get to town. Sheriff, I wet myself rockin' on your knee. And Rat, you just can't believe I could ever hurt Pop! That man was like a favorite uncle. I used to ride on his horse with him, and later on in his stagecoach—for free."

"Makes your killin' him all the worst," Cathcart declared.

"Ain't it possible Pop was wrong?" Rat said, gazing hopefully at his companions. "He ain't run anywhere, Sheriff. He's give us no fight."

"He's a gambler," the sheriff noted. "Knows how sour the odds'd be."

"But you'll admit, Sheriff Cathcart, he sounds mighty convincin'," Charlie Turley remarked. "All he says 'bout helpin' us's true. Hoyt looked kindly on him, too."

"You look to me as if I'm whippin' a rawboned kid, not arrestin' a murderer," Cathcart complained. "You want proof, do you? Well, there's sure to be some hereabouts. Rat, you take Mitch along the river there. You Turleys help me search."

Rat nodded, then motioned Mitch along. The two friends wandered a hundred yards or so down the river before stopping. Mitch turned nervously back toward the hill, and Rat frowned.

"Ain't always possible to keep everything hidden, is it?" Rat asked. "You could mask yer face, but you couldn't change yer voice."

"I can't believe the old man would say it was me."

"I cain't believe it was."

"Then don't, Rat. No jury will. You know yourself I come up here often. Ain't a crime."

"I want to trust you, Mitch, but I saw it all. I know you. I read the truth in yer eyes."

"You only see what you want to see," Mitch muttered bitterly. "I saved your life once."

"I repaid that favor."

"With money. That's the whole trouble, ain't it? I took some money off you, and that Becky Cathcart ain't had a good word for me since. Soured her pa, too. Now Pop gets shot, and I'm handy to blame!"

"Stop it!" Rat shouted, covering his eyes. "Why don't you run?"

"Run where?" he asked. "I'd be posted all over Texas. What chance would I have? I'm no loner, Rat. I need people 'round to ply my trade. I got no sharpshooter's eye, and I ain't quick. Some bounty man'd shoot me inside a week."

"If you owned up to it, maybe . . ."

"They'd let me go? You know Lem Cathcart," Mitch said, grinding his teeth. "Ever know him to ease the law's bite?"

Voices called from the camp then, and Rat motioned for Mitch to turn back. They returned slowly, deliberately. Rat kept expecting Mitch to speak, but he didn't. They met the sheriff under the shade of the white oak. Clem Turley then held up a flour sack filled with bank notes. Holes for eyes had been carefully cut.

"The mask," Rat said, sighing.

"So?" Mitch cried. "I never seen that thing."

"You kilt Hoyt," Clem accused.

"I couldn't," Mitch insisted. "Rat, think about it. You saw me in Albany when you headed out, didn't you? I was still in town at midday, playin' cards. When did the Oxenbergs hit you? I was in Albany."

"Rat?" the sheriff asked, eyeing Rat nervously. Mitch gazed with equally intense eyes. Honor and betrayal seemed muddled. Somewhere in between justice shouted its name. And Pop howled for revenge.

"Look at his boots, Rat," the sheriff suggested. "Been scrubbed, I see, but I'd bet my life that's blood stainin' his shirt."

"I cut myself," Mitch claimed.

"Where?" Rat asked.

"His gun's been cleaned, but you can smell powder on his clothes," the sheriff pointed out. "The trail heads right here."

It was Rat's turn to stare at Mitch. The accusing eyes seemed to bore right through him.

"He had time to follow you east, didn't he?" Cathcart asked.

"He could've followed," Rat muttered.

"Rat?" Mitch asked, dropping his chin into his hands.

"Why?" Rat demanded. "Why?"

"How else was I goin' to get the money," Mitch mumbled. "I ain't had no luck at cards. Oren said all I'd do is note your leavin' and trail along. He promised me three-hundred dollars."

"And he paid you, didn't he?" Cathcart said, grabbing Mitch by his shirt and throwing him to the ground. "Surprised there wasn't a bonus for killin' Pop."

"Did you tell 'em how Efrem and I argued against killin' you?" Mitch asked. "Ask Ef. He'd attest to me just comin' along the one time."

"He's dead," Rat answered.

"So're you, Mitch," Clem declared.

"Lord, this is sure to kill his ma," Charlie added. "Good woman like her! Her one boy gone bad, and the whole town knowin' it."

"Ain't there a way to do it so Mary don't have to know?" Clem asked, staring at the white oak.

"Well, he's as good as confessed to doin' it," Cathcart noted. "Plainly guilty. Waste o' time, takin' him to trial. Bein' locked up in that oven of a jail's just torture. Cruel to him and his folks both. Might as well get it done right here and now."

"What?" Mitch shouted.

"I got a good rope," Clem mumbled. "I'll fetch it."

"You can't," Rat argued. "Not like this! Not here!"

"It's best," Sheriff Cathcart argued.

Clem tossed one end of the rope over a huge branch eight feet or so off the ground. Mitch gazed at the tree, then plunged his face into his hands and sobbed.

"Rat, tell 'em they can't do this," Mitch begged. "They'd listen to you. I saved your life!"

"Stop whimperin', you worthless excuse for a man!" Cathcart demanded. "Hoyt Palmer left a wife and three kids! What'd he ever do to you save lend you saddle horses and take you for free rides in the summer?"

The Turleys secured the rope to the white oak's trunk. Then Clem began forming a noose in the end that dangled from the tree.

"This ain't right," Rat declared, stepping past Mitch to confront Lem Cathcart. "Ought to be a trial. It ain't all black and white. Could be a judge'd see it different. Mitch is due a chance."

"Sure, he is," the sheriff agreed. "The same sort o' chance he give Hoyt Palmer. You remember him, don't you, Rat? Told you to call him Pop and treated you like an extra son. Took you in, made a place for you in his own family. Forgot that, didn't you?"

"Before I even knew Pop Palmer, the Morrises opened their door and welcomed me inside," Rat reminded Cathcart. "You recall 'cause I was at yer house then. Wasn't anybody else save Otto Plank'd take me. It was Mitch asked 'em."

"I know you feel a debt to Mitch, and to the Morrises, too, Rat, but puttin' this off'd be poor service to any o' them. Mitch'd only see a whole town starin' up when he walked to the gallows. As for John and Mary, how do you suppose they'd feel seein' their own boy paraded down Main Street, a thief and a murderer? Think on that, Rat Hadley. Like as not it'd kill 'em both. Some thanks you'd hand 'em."

"You mean to hang him and just forget it ever happened?" Rat asked. "Never tell anybody?"

"Cain't you see that's best?" Clem asked.

"A real kindness," Charlie added. "Mitch, you got to see that yourself. Erases the slate, so to speak. Nobody 'cept us'll know."

"That bein' the case," Mitch said, swallowing his tears and rising to his feet, "why not just turn 'round and let me go? I promise I'll ride so far north you'll never hear a whisper 'bout me in the future. I'll disappear."

"You done wrong," Cathcart barked, glaring at the young outlaw with stone-cold eyes. "Got to pay for it."

"Rat?"

Rat couldn't answer. He turned away, but Mitch called to him again.

"Sheriff, when'll you do it?" Mitch asked.

"I figured straight away. You need some time, do you?"

"Yessir," Mitch said, steadying himself. "An hour?"

"Got your watch, Charlie?" Clem asked. "Time him. Maybe we can dig a grave."

"Rat'll show you where," Mitch said. "Just the other side o' yon oak. Near where Boswell lies."

"Who?" Clem asked.

"An old friend," Rat muttered. "One we never met."

The sheriff flashed them a confused look, but Rat refused to share the tale. Instead he drew Mitch aside, and the two of them sat together and recounted old times.

"Ain't yer doin', Rat," Mitch said, leaning against his old friend. "Just old Boswell's luck come home to roost."

"Guess so," Rat said, shuddering. "Always thought I was the one to catch the hard breaks."

"Maybe that's what put the backbone in you, Rat. Lord knows I never had any."

"Mitch, you had plenty. Ain't many boys'd stand up to Otto Plank when he had a shotgun in his hands."

"I had room to run," Mitch muttered. "You never did. You swear you won't let on to Ma and Pa. Tell 'em I went off to Kansas. I spoke of it."

"I will."

"Promise?"

"Yes, Mitch. And I'll see the others do the same."

"That's a burden lifted, at least. You got yourself some more reward comin', I expect. Guess that'll have to do. Sheriff ain't apt to give you the three hundred."

"No," Rat agreed.

Mitch stared silently at the white oak then, and except for making a brief nature call, he remained still and quiet as the minutes passed relentlessly on.

"Can I get you somethin'?" Rat asked when the Turleys led a horse toward the tree. "I think Charlie's got a bottle."

"Can't drink nothin'," Mitch said. "I seen a man hung once. Wet himself."

"I imagine he was past carin' then, Mitch."

"You'd remember it, though. Rat, I take it hardest you seein' me cry. And knowin' the worst."

"It won't be what I remember," Rat assured his old friend. "I'll only think o' the very best."

"That's more comfort'n you can know."

The Turleys took charge of Mitch thereafter, and Rat stepped away. He lacked the courage to watch.

"Sheriff, you sure you couldn't look the other way a minute?" Mitch asked as Clem bound his hands. "Only take me a minute."

"Make peace with the maker, Mitch," Cathcart urged. "Won't be another chance."

It was then, as the Turleys placed the noose around the quivering young man's neck and hauled him atop his nervous horse, that Mitch's face paled.

"Lord, you really aim to do this, don't you?" he shouted.

"Man's got to pay for his wrongs," the sheriff insisted.

"A man?" Mitch cried. "I ain't but twenty. Shoot, look at me! I ain't full growed!"

"Grow some backbone," Clem urged.

"You go to blazes!" Mitch growled. "Look at me, you men. I'm about to die at your hands. Look at me, Rat!"

Rat turned and gazed upon a man gone mad. Mitch's eyes seemed to blaze with sudden hatred.

"Damn you all," Mitch muttered. "And damn this place. If I got to die here, then I curse the life out o' this place. May nothin' grow here ever again. And . . ."

Mitch never finished. Clem Turley slapped the horse's rump, and the animal sped away, leaving Mitch dangling by the rope. He coughed and kicked and died.

Rat was transfixed by the glassy glimmer in Mitch's eyes. Life had slipped away. It hadn't walked softly into a fog as his mother had once described it. No, death had come like a thief to snatch Mitch's essence.

"Cut him down," Sheriff Cathcart instructed.

Charlie reached up and slashed the rope. Clem dragged Mitch to the open grave and dumped him in like so much useless fodder.

"I'll do that," Rat said when the Turleys started to kick dirt over Mitch. "I know how he'd want it."

"No markers," Cathcart insisted.

"No name," Rat argued. "Only fittin' there's a marker."

"All right," the sheriff agreed. "Should we wait on you?"

"No, go ahead," Rat urged. "I got some peace to find."

"Here?" Clem asked, staring nervously at the dangling rope.

"It's as good a place as any," Rat told them. "I'll see you all in Thayerville."

"Sure, son," Cathcart said as he turned to leave. "Be back in time for supper, though."

"I will," Rat pledged.

Epilogue

Five years had passed since Erastus Hadley had gently eased dirt over the features of the best friend he would ever have. The grave had been outlined in gray limestone rocks, and Erastus had erected a marker with the simple epitaph FRIEND carved with a knife. Wind or visitors had carried off the plank by summer, and gradually the rocks had rolled away. Nature had its way of accepting the dead, taking them to her heart.

The white oak lost its leaves that next fall, but they didn't return in April as before. Thistle and briars grew by that tree, and pencil cactus, too. The grasses and the wildflowers vanished, and the tree turned ghostly white. Perhaps it was Mitch's curse killed the giant white oak. Or maybe time caught up with the place as it did all things. Erastus Hadley didn't know. Years had passed since he'd buried his father on another hill, and he'd seldom since searched for answers or expected to find any.

He'd returned to Thayerville as promised, in time for supper. Afterward

Becky had led him out to the porch, and they made their peace. They were married under an August moon, and Erastus had used his share of the reward to purchase the old Plank place. It seemed right somehow that such a dark, haunted sort of place should see new beginnings.

Erastus never had the heart to ride guard for the Western Stage again, and he instead accepted a deputy's badge. He wore it three years until the horse and cattle markets revived, and his hands turned to their first love— breeding ponies. He ran a few hundred head of cattle as well, and Becky planted the largest garden in the county. Three children were born in turn, and the youngest was called Mitchell.

"I wonder what ever became of Mitch Morris," Becky often remarked. Thereafter she and Erastus would make up tales of the mysterious gambler to amuse the children. Erastus never shared the truth.

"I only hope he found some peace," he would confide to Becky.

"Have you?" she'd ask.

"Long since," he always answered. "You should know. You brought it to me."